STRANGE TALES OF THE MACABRE: POST-APOCALYPTIC

STRANGE TALES OF THE MACABRE: POST-APOCALYPTIC

Edited by Eric J. Guignard

5X5 PUBLISHING
DREAMLAND, USA

Edited by Eric J. Guignard
Interior layout by Eric J. Guignard
www.ericjguignard.com

Cover layout by John Palisano
www.johnpalisano.com

Cover art by Greg Chapman
https://darkartiste.wordpress.com

"Silent Passenger" © 2018 by Kate Jonez. First published in *18 Wheels of Science Fiction: A Long Haul into the Fantastic*, edited by Eric Miller, Big Time Books.

"Ruminations" © 2014 by Rena Mason. First published in *Qualia Nous*, edited by Michael Bailey, Written Backwards.

"Down but Not out at the End of the World" © 2016 by Lisa Morton. First published in *Silent Screams: An Anthology of Socially Conscious Dark Fiction*, edited by Josh Strnad, Serpent & Dove Speculative Fiction.

"The Ruiners" (previously named: "All These Things We Didn't Believe" © 2016 by John Palisano. First published in *Snowpocalypse: Tales of the End of the World*, edited by Clint Collins and Scott Woodward, Black Mirror Press.

"Last Night . . ." © 2015 by Eric J. Guignard. First published in *Mark of the Beast: A Collection of Werewolf Stories*, edited by Scott David Aniolowski, Chaosium, Inc.

"Car Trip Bingo" © 2015 by Eric J. Guignard. First published in *SQ Mag*, issue #22, August, IFWG Publishing Australia.

First edition published in August, 2019
ISBN-13: 978-1-949491-15-9 (paperback)
ISBN-13: 978-1-949491-14-2 (e-book)

5X5 PUBLISHING
Dreamland, USA
Made in the United States of America

(V081319)

PART OF A FIVE-VOLUME SERIES:
STRANGE TALES OF THE MACABRE

Strange Tales of the Macabre: Ghosts
edited by Lisa Morton

Strange Tales of the Macabre: Gothic
edited by John Palisano

Strange Tales of the Macabre: Haunted Journeys
edited by Rena Mason

Strange Tales of the Macabre: Post-Apocalyptic
edited by Eric J. Guignard

Strange Tales of the Macabre: Stormy Weather
edited by Kate Jonez

TABLE OF CONTENTS

INTRODUCTION: ONE VOICE OF THE MACABRE

by Eric J. Guignard

T HE THING OF IT IS, I *LOVE* STORIES SET IN A post-apocalyptic world.

It doesn't matter if the tone of stories are utopian (rebuilding a hopeful or "better" future) or dystopian (imaginings of something very bleak or terrifying that might occur), or whether the setting is something quite subtle and near to looming over our current lives, or else it's a vision of millennia far from now, the fact remains, simply, I love the post-apocalyptic.

I don't know why this is, that I've always been drawn to this genre of fiction, except to think it speaks to some desire to build, to create, or in the case of post-apocalypse to *re-create* out of rubble or of what once was, while in possession of only tenacity and a few meager trappings. Which I think, also, is the act of writing itself, the desire to create something out of nothing, or else (at least) the rubble of something that once was.

Every time an author ends one story and begins another, a small apocalypse has occurred for them, the dissolution of one world that they've built in order to begin building another world, another idea, another set of lives and rules and conflicts . . . and if it just happens to include disasters or monsters or villains, so much the better.

Post-apocalyptic fiction is all about survival as well as the need for adaptability, not to mention the *necessity* for a creative spirit. And creative spirits are what you will find herein.

Whether Kate Jonez's reflections of a technologically empathetic companion, or Rena Mason's vision of living in a war-torn nation; whether Lisa Morton's survival-fueled flight from hungry hunters, or John Palisano's terrifying yet redemptive tale of weather-born invaders; or whether my own takes of a world caught suddenly by a moon that no longer moves, or else a car trip through a landscape of post-apocalyptic sights; within this book thrills, chills, and a plenitude of wonder await.

Of course it is also my sincerest hope that if you enjoy this volume, you will seek out the other volumes in this series. Helmed by Lisa Morton, we five writers sought a way to share our work amongst themes that excited each of us. Lisa took *Ghosts* (her forté), John selected *Gothic*, Kate slotted *Stormy Weather*, and Rena culled *Haunted Journeys*. My own choice was obvious and immediate.

But whether a bump in the night, a bolt of lightning across the sky, or a reflection that moves on its own, all these writings, these stories from each volume, born from worlds heaving and tumultuous, they are all **STRANGE TALES OF THE MACABRE.**

Midnight cheers,

—Eric J. Guignard
Chino Hills, California
June 21, 2019

SILENT PASSENGER

BY KATE JONEZ

T HE TWINGE IN JERRI-LYNN'S EYE TOOTH GOES OFF like a siren, more a sound than a pain.

The suit standing at the break room whiteboard under the unforgiving eye of the LED lights doesn't hear it. Of course, there's no reason he would. Jerri-Lynn knows this on an intellectual level, but the sensation of pain is so present in the world it seems unbelievable that no one else can perceive it.

The suit keeps on talking and pointing with his laser like nothing is wrong. "The neural networks of the processor power the mechanism by pulling energy from objects moving in a co-equal direction." Zip, zip with the laser pointer.

What does that even mean? Jerri-Lynn feels stupid. She suspects the words are chosen for that very purpose. *Neural networks—processor—co-equal.* Technical words, manly slang. She could figure it out if she tried. She'd deciphered the language of trucks. *Solenoid—drivetrain—S-cam.* It isn't that hard once the top layer is peeled back.

"When objects move in a dis-equal direction they decrease the efficiency of propulsion by twenty-five percent, thus effectuating a need for additional propulsion—" The suit turns and swirls the laser in front of each of them as though they might chase it like cats, then finishes with a dramatic flourish, "i.e. drivers."

Dis-equal—propulsion—effectuating. Jerri-Lynn could look up the words. Ask the questions everyone has, but no one is asking. Her heart isn't in it. She doesn't want to learn anything new that she'll never use again after this one last run. She should probably care more, but she's more concerned about the fact that she can't imagine what she's going to do next. The truck will go. With her for a while, then without her.

The suit's way of speaking is hard and clipped like Italians in movies but with most of the edges filed off. The words he's saying sound practiced. He's not the scientist. He's the pill the scientists want the drivers to swallow. The company probably thinks they'll listen to this thinly disguised tough guy more than an actual intellectual. The guy isn't from Wichita, yet he doesn't have a speck of insecurity about being an outsider. The opposite in fact. His confidence fills the room like expensive cologne. Jerri-Lynn wonders what it would feel like to be that sure of herself. It'd be hard to hate anybody more than the flannel-clad good ole boys in the break room hate this dude. Waves of it waft off them. He isn't fazed at all.

Charlie Mason raises his hand the way kids do in school. It's not a thing a grown man usually has to do, and he's got a look on his face like a dog that made a snack out of the trash.

The suit tilts his chin at him.

Charlie shuffles his feet on the cement floor before he says. "Alright, tell me if I'm understanding this correct. We don't stop for gas no more, right?"

"That's right."

"Why's that again?"

The suit's eyes narrow and he gets a look on his face like he'd whack Charlie with a newspaper if he had one. "You want me to start over from the beginning?"

The guys around the table groan in unison.

Jerrie-Lynn feels like groaning herself but mostly because her tooth is throbbing.

"Nah, don't do that." Charlie takes off his glasses and wipes the lenses on his T-shirt. "I just want to be for sure that I don't have to stop for gas."

"That's right."

Charlie perches his glasses on his nose and squints at the white board.

"Lookit." Bill Pullman grabs a napkin. "You know that joke about how you make a car go by raising up the rear wheels so it's always rolling downhill?"

A few of the guys chuckle then choke it off when they realize they're laughing at Charlie's expense. Before the new management took over, Pullman never talked much in the break room being the only black guy on the crew. Seems that times have changed enough that he doesn't have so much to worry about such things anymore.

"Yup," Charlie says.

"It's like that," Pullman says, "only not exactly." He leans back and grabs the marker off the white board tray and scribbles on the napkin. "The trucks get their power from each other and the other vehicles going in the same direction. Like there's a magnet pulling them all along."

The suit comes over and looks at the napkin. He twists his mouth into something like a smile and bobs his head. "Only it's not a magnet."

"Right," Pullman agrees. "Just an analogy."

Jerri-Lynn still doesn't get it. She doesn't really understand why she has to. Men like to know stuff even if it doesn't change a thing.

"Then how come it's different on County 287?" Jerri-Lynn asks. "They don't have the magnets put in yet?"

Pullman gives her an exasperated look.

"There aren't any magnets," the suit snaps like she's said the stupidest thing ever.

She should have kept her mouth shut.

"Yeah, I don't get it either," Charlie says.

Pullman draws a bunch of lines on the napkin. "Because County 287 is two lanes in each direction and the vehicles going east drag down on the vehicles going west instead of giving them power.

"Yeah and . . . " Charlie says.

"It's a bug," Pullman says. "And we got to help the trucks by giving the power to get to the four-lane road."

"Hmmph." Charlie grumbles. "Might well as use gas."

"You bought any gas in a while, pal?" the suit says in his testy way. "Costs as much as the load you're carrying." He turns back to the white board.

"Like solar panels made of people." Pullman says, grinning at his own wit.

Pain is punishment.

Jerri-Lynn isn't sure what she's being punished for. Could be a lot of things. Most likely eating a donut for breakfast one too many days. She wants to get up from the table and get an aspirin, or whatever, from the drawer under the coffee machine, but she doesn't want to draw attention to herself. Ever since most of the regular crew had gotten laid off, the spotlight has been on her. Everyone thinks she was one of the chosen few for politically correct reasons. She's the only female in the room. And years of experience have taught her never to shine a light on that.

The suit keeps on with his lesson like Pullman didn't even explain it better. When he gets to the part about the IRL beta testing, the thought that saying "in real life" takes exactly as much effort as saying the initials causes another siren of pain to shudder through Jerri-Lynn. This convinces her to get the aspirin anyway. She slides her chair across the floor, rolls her shoulders forward and makes her way as unobtrusively as she can to the medicine drawer.

"Don't leave now." The suit says flashing a mouthful of brilliant white teeth. "I'm just getting to the part where you get paid to coast."

The guys around the table rub their stubbly chins and chuckle in fake solidarity with the suit, even Pullman who should know better. Jerri-Lynn has a reputation for coasting. There's always rumors like that whenever a woman has a man's job. There's no way the suit would know what the good ole boys say, but it makes the joke richer. Anyway, there's probably some truth to it. She's not adverse to doing things the easy way.

We are all Judases now. No one is any better off than anyone else. Those of us holding on to the tail end of how things used to be, we're worse than scabs ever were. We're not only betraying our fellow drivers, we are species traitors. Laugh harder, sons of bitches. Not long from now you won't have to complain about women taking what's yours anymore. These machines are going to be the end of us for good. The suit doesn't know it, but it's just a matter of time before they come for him too. We're all fucked. We're all good and fucked.

Jerri-Lynn doesn't feel as bad about the situation as she probably should. It's been a good long time since she's felt anything one way or the other about the state of her life. Now the good ole boys are up the same creek without a paddle. That's okay by her. Misery love company as Jim used to say.

She hadn't thought twice about signing on for this job. It had been the right thing to do. She's got bills. She's got plenty of those. It's her only choice really. Work is the only thing that holds the void at bay.

She should have paid the extra twenty-five dollars per pay period for dental and seen the dentist already. This toothache is going to cost a fortune and chances are her insurance won't be around after this last run.

She shakes out three pills from the bottle, swallows two and presses one against the depression in her eye tooth.

"All right," the suit says. "Enough theory. Time to get this party started."

Jerri-Lynn takes a swig of burned coffee from the bottom of the pot, tosses the cup in the trash, and follows the group into the harsh artificial sun of the garage. The truck in her bay looks like any other she's driven lately. She hopes she doesn't have a load of liquor this time. Road bandits seem to be able to sniff that prize out from miles away. If she's hauling liquor, she'll have to take extra precautions to keep from getting herself robbed. That'll mean no rest stops after dark and generally less freedom. No use worrying, though, she'll get the manifest soon enough.

She'd like to be on the road already. Sitting idle makes her itchy. All this talk with white boards and pointers and interaction with people she'd rather not talk to is exactly the kinds of stuff that made her quit her office job and become a driver all those years ago. Jim never liked the idea. But he should have thought about that before enlisting. Jerri-Lynn never like the idea of him going to some off the map to a mountain in the middle of nowhere to play with guns either. He hadn't listened to her, so she hadn't listened to him. The twinge in her heart reminds her that she once thought fighting Jim was a good idea.

Jerri-Lynn climbs up into the cab. It looks enough like every other truck she's ever driven since she had to sell her own to cover expenses, so she feels confident she can do the job. *Expenses* is not a word that really covers what she lost . . . The thought she's doing all she can to hold off the memories send an ache through her as sharp as the sensation in her tooth. Pain is a reminder. The worst has already come to pass.

She climbs up into the cab, grabs the tablet with the manifest, and flicks it on. Liquor of course.

There's a few odd things in the cab. A rubber nipple that fits on her index finger like a condom and a strap that goes around her chest. The gear shift is disturbingly simplified. It looks like a Frankenstein switch. Down for dead. Up for electrified, but other than that, things are the same. Jerri-Lynn straps herself in and rolls down the window.

"Ready to roll!" the suit says with way too much enthusiasm. He weaves through the lineup flashing his bright smile and nodding at the drivers. The artificial light glints off his too-groomed hair making him seem unreal somehow, as though he too is made of metal and technology.

One after another, doors roll up and the trucks slide out into the pale morning light. Jerri-Lynn grabs the gear shift and drags it into the *electrified* position. No engine rumble rattles the cab, but there's an ever-so-slight tightening in the chest strap. All the dash lights come on to let her know the truck is ready to go. She depresses the floor pedal and the truck glides soundlessly onto the road.

The suit yells some technical gibberish at Jerri-Lynn that she ignores as she turns out of the lot and pulls onto the feeder road to County 287. She's in control of the rig. She was afraid maybe it would steer itself and she'd be at its mercy. That comes later, she thinks bitterly. She accelerates up the access road. No matter how hard she depresses the pedal the speed gauge won't go above 63.

The morning is sweater cool and the sky is an enormous expanse of cloudless blue, the kind of weather that tricked her into to thinking she was going to like Wichita when she and Jim moved into their first apartment by the Air Force base. She'd liked the town back then, but she would have been happy anywhere, in the middle of the desert even, when she and Jim first got married. He was a force in her that weather couldn't touch. With him gone, she's on shaky ground. She feels acutely how much of an outsider she'd managed to remain. In ten years she hadn't gotten to know much about the place at all. Of course, she knows which way the streets go, how to get to the grocery store, what the local TV channels are, but she'd never bothered to make Wichita home. Ten years really flies by.

She's greeted by the sign that lets her know the distance to Lawton, to Childress, to Amarillo, dusty western towns rich in rugged history and lore. Like most places in Texas they are built for the locals. They hide all their secrets from people just passing through. Amarillo is where the 287 meets the interstate I-40. Amarillo is where the machine takes over and Jerri-Lynn coasts. Two-hundred miles or so, and she can coast.

Jerri-Lynn wishes she'd stopped at the Beverly Liquor on the outskirts of town and picked up two pints from Jorge. Seems almost a crime not to stop in and say good-bye to one of the few people on earth who know her by name on what would probably be her last run. She should have signed up with that other outfit when she had the chance. Too late for regrets now. Hopefully, she won't land in a dry county by nightfall. She is going to need something to dull the ache tonight. All the aches. She puts her tongue in the depression in her tooth. Sometimes dulling the pain is the only option. On an ordinary haul she'd know exactly how far she could go in a day. With the machine in control there is no telling where she'll land.

Miles of ranch land littered with pump jacks that don't know they are living in their end times fly by. Jerri-Lynn turns on the radio and pushes seek until she lands on a call-in show out of Lawton. The signal won't last long, but she likes getting a peek into the guts of a place. They give up their secrets on these radio shows. She wonders if they know that.

Solitude is the best part of driving. The suspended place between leaving and arriving is a vacation from the job of living. All work is like that, Jerri-Lynn thinks in a moment of clarity. That's why so many people neglect everything else for it. It's good to have a purpose, if only for a while.

Jerri-Lynn doesn't bother to pass the cars and other trucks. 63 miles per hour is not fast enough to get around any but the oldest jalopy. The throb in her tooth has dulled to the point that it's bearable if not comfortable. If it was like this all the time, she could probably skip the dentist.

Pain is a warning.

The pain will be back with a fury, Jerri-Lynn knows. It is just a matter of biting down on some sweet thing or breathing in cold air. That's how pain is. Whether Jerri-Lynn uncovers its true nature and purpose or not, one thing she is sure of, it will definitely be back. Would have been nice if Jim could have figured out that one fact. He'd chased the cure like he was going to put an end to it for good. His persistence is what got him in the end.

Thoughts of Jim threaten to saw into her and slice her open laying bare all her raw nerves. Gone is gone. It's better to put him out of her mind. She's already thought about every detail of what went wrong for months on top of months and that got her nowhere. *What if he'd talked about the IED that had blown up his friend and irreparably twisted his spine? What if a different doctor prescribed less dangerous medicine? What if she'd been kinder, or tougher, or different in some way? What if she'd followed him around and discovered what he'd been up to in the months before everything went wrong instead of trusting the lies of a man in the grip of an irresistible pain?* Re-hashing the details never changes a thing. Jerri-Lynn settles into the road hum with its vibration under her feet and lets the rig carry her into the space between leaving and arriving.

The lilt of the Texoma twang punctuated by staccato bursts of homestyle swearing about football or Oklahoma City politics buzzes from the radio like an especially docile horsefly not really annoying enough to do anything about. Jerri-Lynn eats mile after mile of white dashes and stripes without thinking about much of anything. The throb in her tooth flares just enough to keep her from getting comfortable.

"Jerri!"

Jerri-Lynn jumps. The voice slashes through the white noise of her thoughts. Jim's voice. Unmistakable.

"Pull over," Jim's voice demands. It's only his voice, not him. It can't possibly be him. He's gone. Of that one thing she's sure.

She twists her head from side to side. She's alone in the cab. Instinctively, she slams her palm into all the radio buttons at once. The talk radio voices fall silent. She grips the wheel, leans into it, listens.

"Pull over."

The voice is impossibly tangible like a crack of lightning in the middle of the night that blows sleep away. She is compelled to hear it. Even though it can't be a real thing. Can't possibly be.

JCT I-40 Amarillo 3 MILES. The sign flashes in front of her eyes.

Impossible. Where had two hundred miles and three hours gone? That is a lot to lose.

The strap around her chest compresses enough for her to notice but not enough to be uncomfortable. It feels disturbingly like a hug.

Alongside the road a man wearing jeans with the creases ironed in and a thin jacket over a pristine white T-shirt waves her down. He doesn't seem agitated. His motions are controlled, in fact, perfunctory, as though he's been waiting for her.

Jerri-Lynn's heart skips a beat. The strap tries to sooth her with another hug. This man cannot possibly be who he appears to be. He's stepped out of the time where ironed creases in blue jeans were in fashion, a time when a young soldier could believe in things. She's projecting her memories onto the blank canvas of a hitchhiker. That's the only explanation. When she pulls the wheels onto the sandy shoulder, the rubber nipple on her index finger contracts. The rig knows she's decelerating. The rig knows.

Passengers are strictly forbidden. Jerri-Lynn has no doubt this transgression will be thoroughly recorded by all the devices that must surely be standard in a vehicle like this. She's not deterred by half-remembered rules. This is her last run; the rules are unfurling before her like dice tumbling down a craps table.

She rolls to a stop.

Jim's revenant shoulders a duffle bag, runs to the door, and pulls it open. A gust of winter air heavy with the arid scent of scrub wood and the dug earth of gopher burrows but with top notes of asphalt and exhaust blows over her. She breathes in the chill of it. The siren of her toothache sounds. He climbs in without asking her destination or any of the usual questions a rider would. In spite of the fact that such things are impossible, it's as though he actually is Jim and not just the conjured image of the specter who's been riding with her since she found herself all alone. The resemblance is remarkable. Even the smell of him is Jim's.

"Hey," he says when he settles in. He runs his hand over the brush of his close-cropped hair.

The ache in Jerri-Lynn radiates all through her tainting everything close by.

"I'm taking the I-40 west as far as it goes," Jerri-Lynn says. This is the first time she's thought about her destination. It's a black hole, the future, once this last run is done. A foreign landscape she doesn't have the will to understand. Electronic language is on the verge of rendering her illiterate in a world she once navigated with ease. She'd almost rather go into it blind.

Jim doesn't respond. In every way he's the silent rider by her side.

Jerri-Lynn electrifies the lever, depresses the gas, and the rig pulls onto the highway. The sequence that initiates motion in so many tons of metal is too easy somehow as if the truck has a will to be in motion and is making things as easy as possible.

"Where are you coming from?" Jerri-Lynn asks as the last few miles of County Road 287 fly by.

The passenger turns, looks at her with his blank canvas face. "It's where I'm going that counts."

He's right about that. Jim is right about that. Jerri-Lynn yearns to believe her man is beside her again. She wants to fall into the dream, but she's afraid to reach out, to touch him. She fears that the tenuous illusion might disintegrate, and she'd find herself touching some random man she found alongside the road.

"Well, where are you going, then?"

"I'm going where you're going," Jim says. "Where is it you want to go?"

She pushes the button for the radio. A Waylon song, with a scratch in the same place as her old vinyl copy, conjures up the weight of the down-filled sleeping bag, the crackle of the campfire, the bullfrogs at dusk along the Red River on their first camping trip floods the cab.

Jim crooks his lopsided smile at her. "I remember that trip like it was yesterday."

"You remember?"

"I remember what you remember."

How is that possible? Jerri-Lynn tenses up like the pain is going to return. She waits for it. There's a saying about things that are too good to be true. She puts her tongue on the indention on her eye tooth and still the pain doesn't come.

"Are you a ghost?" Jerri-Lynn asks. She doesn't really need an answer. Nothing will change if she knows or she doesn't. She should keep her eyes on the road, but that probably doesn't matter either. She stares at Jim, taking in every detail.

The rig gives her a reassuring squeeze as the red, white, and blue sign for the I-40 turn off sails into view. Jerri-Lynn doesn't need the sign to tell her she's reached the end of the road where she's needed. The wide-open expanses of earth, sky, cow trails, and mesquite brush of the county road veer into a tangle of steel and concrete and asphalt. All that's left for her to do is to steer one last time onto the interstate and hand over the reins to the machine.

"We've come to the place." Jim's voice has a metallic edge.

Jerri-Lynn squints hard at him. She can't decide if she's squinting to see beyond the illusion or if she's squinting to hold it together. She had feared Jim was an illusion, but she's amazed by how much she wants him to be real.

"We don't need you anymore." The voice coming from Jim's mouth resonates and reverberates in a way no human voice can. It's machine-like, but it isn't unkind. "We don't need you, but we gain nothing from your suffering."

"You'll let me have Jim?" Jerri-Lynn's voice quavers. She's never wanted anything more.

Jim grins his cockeyed grin and his eyes flash with the glint of mischief Jerri-Lynn had always loved. "Yes," he says in a voice that's all his.

As the exchange begins, a thrum and a rumble emanate from the guts of the truck. If Jerri-Lynn had been in control of an ordinary rig, she might have pulled over to check out what was going wrong. But she's not in control. She doesn't worry because whether she understands or not the outcome remains the same. The sound swells and the vibration of it becomes a solid thing like the gravity that pushes back on a roller coaster rider. The magnet, if it is a magnet, or maybe it's bugs in the system, pulls and pushes on her from all directions. It feels like bugs inside her scurrying to get out whatever way they can.

She squeezes Jim's hand and squints to see beyond the illusion of him as the inescapable sound compresses him. She fears he'll become two-dimensional.

The rig travels at a speed Jerri-Lynn can't comprehend. Digital displays on the dash are an indecipherable blur of symbols she's never learned. Through the windshield, the view is a smear, of what she's not sure. The signs and symbols of driving she knows so well have become something entirely different. She's in a foreign land.

At the moment this thought occurs to her, the scene before her shifts. The blur of rushing motion settles. The unbearable thrum becomes birds singing and crickets chirping. Prairie grass waves like it does on a spring day when it's finally warm enough for the creek to set the tadpoles free. Jerri-Lynne knows she's hooked up as a battery to some kind of magnetic future machine but that's not how it seems at all. She mashes the clutch and downshifts to second. For some inexplicable reason the pickup she and Jim bought used just after they got married is bumping along a dirt path down to the Red River. She reaches out and takes Jim's hand. It's as warm to the touch as ever it ever was. "You don't have to feel no pain," Waylon wails from the radio. The only thing she knows for sure is all *her* pain is gone.

Every last bit.

RUMINATIONS

BY RENA MASON

RUNNING LATE TO CATCH THE BUS, LUISA KICKED a raised part of the sidewalk toes first.

"*Mierda!*" She winced but managed to keep her balance. She stopped, raised her leg, and massaged her big toe through her canvas work shoes. Relieved to feel no broken bones, she lowered her foot, ignored the pain, and hurried to the bus stop.

She shouldn't have tripped, but that's what happens when you're not paying attention. After walking the same way to work for the past eight months, she'd memorized every crack and weed in the three hundred eighty-six square concrete slabs from her apartment building to the covered bench where she sat and waited most days. Today, she woke up late after dreaming of the warring city, and keeping to a strict daily routine had been what saved her. The bus driver, a friendly middle-aged man named Toby, had waited for her with the door open.

"Thank you," she gasped.

Toby smiled. "Saw you coming. How's your foot?"

"It's okay. Thanks."

"Good."

He closed the door behind her and pulled away from the curb. She went to her usual spot on the bus, always empty an hour before sunrise. Nine rows back, opposite from where Toby sat, Luisa sidestepped her way to the window seat and plopped down. She pulled her hurt foot out of the shoe and examined the stubbed toe. Dark purplish blood spread out underneath most of the nail bed in the shape of a cloud. She shook her head, knowing the dead nail would eventually peel off on its own, leaving her with a raw, fragile toe. Luisa looked to the right at her reflection in the glass.

"See what you made me do?" she whispered.

Four months ago, Luisa noticed a girl who mimicked her every move in the window. The reflection looked much like her own, only younger, a girl in her late twenties maybe. She had a bleak expression and fear in her eyes. It took two weeks of experimenting to convince herself the anomaly was real and not a trick of her mind or wishful thinking. She'd taken a mirrored compact from her purse and looked into it, glanced at the bus window and back again. The reflected images differed from one another. In her compact, she saw herself as she should be: a 48-year-old widower from Guatemala, lucky to get a job at her age for financial support. A woman with two sons, both adults in constant trouble with the law and presently serving time in the California prison system. For her own good and sanity, she didn't keep in touch, disappeared from their lives. Life would've been different if she'd had a daughter.

Sadness showed on her face, but didn't compare to the young girl in the window. That girl's eyes expressed a fear she hadn't felt since first arriving in America. All the horrors Luisa had suffered through, she'd left behind in the jungle villages of the old country.

The bus screeched and hissed. It had been still for ten seconds before Toby yelled back:

"Your stop. Number twenty-two."

Her stop had come too quickly. She shoved her foot into the shoe and glanced at the reflection before rising.

"This is your fault, too."

At this rate, she might end up late to work, and that wouldn't be good. Too many others wanted her job. She passed Toby and thanked him.

"You sure you're all right?" he said. "I think that's the first time I've ever had to—"

"Yes, I'm fine." Luisa hurried off the bus.

It would be another twenty-minute walk to the Motel 8 off I-5 near Old Sacramento. Instead of thinking about the younger Luisa, she tried counting cracks in the sidewalk. After five hundred, she gave up and jog-walked the rest of the way.

This must stop. The girl in the window, I won't look at her anymore.

Luisa arrived ten minutes after seven, late for the first time since she got the job. Jan, the shift supervisor, gave her a disappointed look when she handed over the color-coded rooms schedule. Luisa glimpsed the green circular sticker on the upper right corner of the paper and held back a groan. Floors seven through ten, where they checked in most of the families with small children.

"Thank you," Luisa said, but she didn't mean it. "If anyone finishes early, I'll send them up."

Luisa nodded and headed for the service elevator, knowing no one would come. Everyone stalled to avoid helping clean the family rooms. The coveted blue rooms schedule, where single businesspeople checked in, would be sorely missed today. They tended to be the neatest, with short stays, and on the first three floors. Sometimes, the beds hadn't even been slept in.

After loading up with supplies, she grabbed a vacuum and pushed the heavy cart down the hall to her first room. The door opened to a disaster area. Fast food containers with spilled contents lay strewn everywhere. Pasta noodles littered the floor next to the beds, some of them stepped on and smeared into the carpet. On average, it took thirty minutes to clean a blue room. Forty minutes into cleaning the green room, spending most of the time on her hands and knees, Luisa swore she'd never be late again.

While running the vacuum over the carpet, now clear of items too soft or wet for the machine, something black darted across the front of the window to the corner of the room. She jumped a little but kept her balance with a firm grip on the vacuum's rubber handle and continued to work. Ghost shadows often moved past her periphery in the hotel. If she ignored them, they'd go away.

The other girls often told stories about people who'd died in the hotel's rooms and scary things they saw at work during their lunches and over breaks. Luisa didn't listen to them. She kept to herself and stayed away from the gossip. Knowing too much might frighten her and she needed the job. Being isolated from their conversations came with a price, though. Other employees took it the wrong way and stopped inviting her to potlucks and parties. Sometimes, she wished they'd ask her again.

Pushing the vacuum back and forth, she could tell the black thing hadn't moved. A knot of discomfort tightened her gut. The temperature dropped, sending chills down her spine. Maybe if she glanced at it, the ghost would be satisfied and disappear. She backed toward the door with the vacuum in front of her and looked up.

It stood in the corner and pointed at the window.

Luisa crossed herself, shook her head, and prayed in Spanish.

The black thing had a human body. It took a step forward then motioned its other hand for Luisa to come.

Ottaya attempted several sleeping positions while bombs exploded far off to the north of the city. Their decoy transport had worked again, but how long would their luck continue until the rebels caught on? The old woman who'd been coming at night to join the transport caravans for shelter needed Ottaya's help, but also slowed her down. Then every morning she'd be gone again. Ottaya didn't mind showing her the way, even though she didn't quite understand why. Anybody else she might have let fall behind, but something about this woman reminded her of an important thing she couldn't explain.

When the time came to move again by day, the same woman could be seen, but only in the window glass. Ottaya thought in earlier times a different person might have looked back at her, someone younger, more familiar, but the memory remained clouded. A lot of war had happened since then, and the glass was always broken now or missing. Recently, she'd made it a point to sit in seats with more intact windows so she might learn more about the woman. But the older lady stared and said nothing.

A loud crash shattered her sleep. The transport went over something that lifted her out of the seat and she banged her head against the metal frame.

She rubbed her temple and opened her eyes.

The older woman looked at her from a glass shard.

How does she get there?

Warm blood trickled down the side of Ottaya's face, which she wiped with her filthy jacket sleeve.

"This is because of you."

"Who are you talking to?" a burly man said from the aisle, hunched over because he was too tall for the transport.

"No one," she said. Then she shouted to the driver. "What is it, Deegan?"

"Road block. They're coming on."

Ottaya rolled her eyes and pushed up her sleeve while the tall man went back to where he'd been sitting. A tattooed barcode appeared on her wrist with the numbers 12-21-9-19-1 imprinted underneath the lines—her resistance identification. Four armed, uniformed men boarded the transport and moved through the rows, checking each passenger. One soldier used a handheld scanner to inspect the barcodes, while the other three had their guns aimed at passengers. Ottaya knew the men wouldn't hesitate to fire if the reader failed to verify a code, even if it was a momentary glitch in the system. She'd seen many innocents of the resistance die this way. When they got to her, she recognized one of them.

"It's good to see you're still alive," he said to her. She nodded.

"Don't move," he said.

The scanner's laser beam read her identification.

Ottaya held her breath and stared into his weapon's muzzle. If something happened, she knew he'd make it quick. When the green light came on, she exhaled.

"You never know," the soldier said, and shrugged—a reminder of how they'd all become indifferent to life and death.

The men moved to the next person. On their way back, the familiar soldier stood next to her and shouted at the driver. "Road bombs ahead. We'll send two cycles in front of you."

Someone in the back groaned.

"I know it doesn't always work, but if the riders stay tight and move fast enough, they could trip a bomb, ride past it and clear the way. It's all we can do," the soldier said. He looked down at Ottaya and smiled.

"Try to keep alive."

"Where is the decoy traveling tonight?"

"You know I can't tell you."

She did, but it never hurt to ask.

"You'll be safe," he said and gripped her shoulder. "We need you in one piece for the genetics module transfer." The soldier released his hold and exited the transport.

My father's memories and knowledge broken down and injected into my brain.

It would happen soon. Ottaya had been mentally preparing for it. Her mind would be a jumbled mess for a day or two, but then she'd have all the knowledge to create the genetic weapons her father had worked on before the rebels eliminated him.

The rebels and resistance had warred for millennia. They'd destroyed many places and then moved on and ruined more. Her father had discovered a way to infect the enemy on a genetic level. A way to break down the chemicals that made them up.

Ottaya looked at the woman in the glass. "My revenge. It's coming."

Engines rattled and shook the transport as the driver put them back in gear. They'd soon be crossing terrain with hidden mines.

She shifted in the seat, feeling anxious and warm. An enormous shadow surrounded them and loomed overhead. Some of the others strained their necks to the side and leaned their heads to look up. An air convoy hovered in the sky above.

Luisa trembled, unable to move, as she stared wide-eyed at the black thing. Her focus remained on its face, and the features became more familiar—the girl from her reflection.

But why was she at the motel? What happened to her?

"*Vas,*" Luisa said. "Go."

The girl from the warring city motioned again for her to come forward. The blackness covering her had once been skin. She had been burned. The char split apart like hard-caked desert floor. Red showed between the cracks—bloody raw flesh. Luisa winced. Perhaps the girl wanted to tell her what happened. Luisa's foot resisted stepping forward. Tears welled in her eyes and she shook her head.

No.

The girl didn't leave. Luisa took several deep breaths trying to compose herself. Maybe she would pass out and the vision would go away. After several minutes of feeling nothing but dizziness and nausea, she looked down at the carpet to avoid seeing the girl. Luisa continued to shake, but keeping her focus elsewhere helped. Only then did her body allow her to step toward the window.

Burnt feet and legs filled her periphery. She lifted her head and stopped. The girl pointed to the window. Luisa felt her body rise from the floor and float closer. Her body came to rest inches from the window with her feet on the carpet.

Reflections moved in the glass, but not the same way they did outside. The images differed. Cars sped across I-5 in the distance, but up close, what she saw in the window confused her. Luisa shifted her focus back and forth between the two scenes, and they didn't make sense.

The reflected landscape had been destroyed; she recognized it now—the warring city. Charred bodies and remnants of an exploded bus littered a road. A large shadow blanketed the scene. A rectangular airplane, like a floating semitrailer, hovered above the carnage. Luisa moved closer, pressed her forehead against the glass.

One of the burnt people came into focus and Luisa gasped. The eyes! They'd been removed, but *after* the body had been burned. The sockets were nothing but dark caverns surrounded by bloody rims, their empty depths extended to the back of the girl's skull. Her brain, everything... gone. Something covered in soot and hardly distinguishable had melded into the palm of the charred woman's hand—a black bag with white stars drawn on it.

"*Como?*" she said, turning to the burnt woman for an answer. No one stood in the corner.

"They've sent an air convoy to protect us," Ottaya said. Two men up front turned around and looked at her.

The man in the back, who'd groaned earlier about the cycles, spoke up. "Oh yeah, I'm sure it's here for me because I dig trenches. Most valuable member of the resistance." He laughed.

His glare bore into her, but Ottaya kept quiet. Yorn had always been a disagreeable bastard, but she didn't feel like getting up and kicking his ass. She rolled her eyes at the others and they grinned, then returned to what they'd been doing. A sudden forward lurch, then back, and the transport traveled on.

Air convoys tended to be inaudible stalking shadows, loaded with weapons, explosives, and soldiers on the ready. The cycles, stripped down for speed, made a high-pitched whirring sound, but so far ahead, they'd be silent. Cyclists had one weapon—a reaper caplet—to be taken if caught by the rebels. Everything remained quiet except for the transport, which needed a new suspension and bounced and squeaked over the bumpy terrain.

A dull pop sounded from the road ahead. The transport jerked to a stop. Everyone stood and looked forward. Plumes of smoke had shot into the air. The air convoy moved forward to investigate. Deeg, the transport driver, turned up his signal receiver.

Loud static, then a voice, "Cyclists triggered mine. Sped past. Both unharmed."

Everyone clapped and cheered.

The tall man looked at Ottaya and winked.

"Stop it," Deegan shouted. "I need the numbers."

When it quieted, the air convoy's navigator relayed land coordinates for Deeg to follow in order to avoid the massive road hole left by the bomb. All fifteen passengers scrambled to find openings to look through when they went around the exploded mess.

Shadows made by the transport stretched farther across the road and crept onto the land. Soon it would be dark. Ottaya knew she'd come—the woman who reminded her of something she did not understand. Her mother had died giving birth; her father disappeared into the laboratories after that. Raised by soldiers, and other members of the resistance who cared for her while her father found a way to destroy the rebels, she knew nothing else.

At the first transport stop, and final checkpoint before leaving again for a safe place to spend the night, Ottaya saw the woman in line. She had something clutched to her chest and a look of fear on her face. The people in front of her had rolled up their sleeves, ready to be scanned.

Before the woman moved, Ottaya approached. The stranger turned to her and spoke in an unfamiliar language. Ottaya took the foreigner by the arm, leaned in, and shushed her. The woman nodded. Together, they walked away from the end of the line to an isolated area around the side of the checkpoint.

The woman whispered gibberish and reached into the bag she had a death grip on earlier. Ottaya paused, and the stranger recognized her hesitation, stopped talking, and smiled. She took something Ottaya had never seen before from a carryall—yellow, long, and curved. The woman pulled the top back and Ottaya jumped a little. This made the stranger giggle, but Ottaya didn't think it funny and would've snapped the woman's neck if she thought her dangerous. The woman peeled the sides down and took a bite, chewed, smiled again, and handed the thing over.

Ottaya took the yellow thing out of respect, smelling it. Slow and cautious at first, she took a few bites, and a pasty sweetness of exotic flavor filled her mouth. Then she devoured the yellow thing with ravenous fervor.

The foreigner smiled and appeared satisfied.

Ottaya reached into her black carryall. She'd used white stones found roadside during one of her transport trips to decorate it with stars. Drawing had always been one of her favorite things to do. Many people of the resistance had complimented her on the beautiful sketches she'd created from the ashes of the ruined cities.

The woman watched and inspected the bag.

A soldier startled both women. He'd been the familiar one. Ottaya didn't know his name, didn't want to. She'd seen too many soldiers disappear from her life, and she liked this one.

"What are you doing over here?" he said. "Helping this woman."

"What is in your hand?"

"The skin of something I ate." Ottaya let it drop to the ground. "It's time to go."

"Can you get us both on the transport?"

"Of course."

Ottaya looked up at the soldier in the most seductive way she knew how. "Without going through the line, I mean."

"But—"

"Please, I'm begging you. It's important. She's with me."

The woman stood silent and unmoving, waiting, as if she had done this before.

"You know I can't." "Then I'll stay here."

"Dammit! You're stubborn." Ottaya smiled.

"Come on, then." The soldier escorted them to the bus with his weapon pointed ahead.

"You look very official," Ottaya said. "What's your name?" "I've seen you for years and now you ask me my name?" "You're helping me. Yes, I'm asking your name?"

"Vinto."

"I like it. Thank you for helping us, Vinto."

"Who is she?" Vinto nodded to the old woman.

"No questions. Maybe I'll tell you after the module injection." "You might forget."

"Then I forget. Maybe you should, too."

None of the other soldiers questioned Vinto when he escorted the two women onto the transport. Ottaya took a seat next to some window glass. No reflection appeared.

Maybe because of the darkness, maybe because she's here.

The foreigner sat next to her and smiled. An hour into the ride, the woman's head rested against her shoulder. She'd fallen asleep, and eventually Ottaya did the same.

Yorn eyed the two from the back and wondered about the strange woman Ottaya had picked up at the checkpoint. For the last few weeks, he'd noticed she had come and gone like a ghost. Perhaps the woman had been sent to further protect Ottaya. He wondered what weapons she carried.

It took Luisa into overtime to finish cleaning the green rooms. No one helped, not even Jan. During lunch, the other women kept to themselves. Luisa spent the entire day working slower than normal and thinking of the young girl. Why had she been burnt, killed—whether or not she came to warn her—or if she'd lost her mind and imagined it all?

With thoughts of the girl on her mind, Luisa almost walked past the bus stop. The deafening rattling of the engine snapped her out of the daze. The late afternoon bus drivers changed every other day. She slid her pass through the reader and chose a different seat than normal, but it didn't matter. Moments later, the younger version of the woman appeared in the glass, uncharred and undamaged. She looked happier. Luisa wondered what made her smile, and knew it wasn't her own reflection. Smiles didn't come often. Happiness was far away, perhaps in a distant past; exhaustion, for sure, but not happiness.

When she got home, Luisa reheated leftovers and ate with the television on, then showered and went to bed. Sleep came late, even though she'd been tired and would've passed out before dinner had it not been for the beeping microwave.

The warring city exploded into her dreams. Bombs and gunfire in the distance. Ruined places. Luisa waiting in line.

The girl took Luisa by the arm and walked her to the side of a building. Soldiers scanned the arms of those at the front of the line. Luisa knew she wouldn't pass. She tried to explain about seeing her burnt ghost, and thank the young doppelganger for protecting her, but in her dreams Luisa spoke Spanish. The people of the warring city spoke a language she'd never heard before.

For the first time in her dreams, Luisa brought her purse. The girl looked thin and hungry, so she'd reached in and found a banana. The girl jumped as Luisa peeled it, which made her laugh. The girl carried a bag, too, but it looked like a backpack for school: black, with white, hand drawn, childlike stars. Luisa somehow knew this girl had been deprived of a childhood, and she wanted to make it right—*the chance to have a daughter*—even if only in her dreams.

One of the soldiers approached and startled them. Luisa could tell he liked the girl, and maybe the girl had felt something for the soldier, too. He helped them bypass the line and onto an old bus with boarded windows and torn seats. In the back, a strange man watched the young girl. Luisa didn't like the way he stared.

Blaring electronic sounds jolted Luisa upright.

The dream-world dissolved as she opened her eyes.

She turned off her alarm clock, then started her daily routine. For the first time since her husband had died, looking around and counting were far from her mind as she made her way to the bus stop. The man at the back of the bus occupied her thoughts—the last bit of dream she remembered. His expression disturbed her.

"You sure you're okay?" Toby said, looking concerned.

Luisa slid her pass and a wave of vertigo forced her to grab the metal handrail.

"Give me a minute."

Luisa recovered and went to her seat, hoping to see the girl. Stars from the vertigo blurred her vision of the window.

Stars! The backpack. The girl dies.

"Aye, *mija,*" she whispered to the glass.

Tears welled and rolled down her cheeks. The thought of losing her dream daughter . . . She touched the cool window.

Where could you be?

She'd been asleep on that old bus before Luisa woke up. If only she could go back and warn her.

Luisa arrived at work before anyone else. Jan had still been working on the rooms schedule when Luisa went into her office.

"You're early," Jan said. "Making up for yesterday."

"Nice job on the green rooms, by the way." "Thank you."

Jan handed her the blue rooms schedule. "Here you go. Early bird gets the worm."

Luisa smiled, but felt disrespected that Jan likened her to a bird eating a worm. She shook her head and left the office.

Every time she'd unlocked one of the doors, Luisa looked in the windows for signs of the girl. All day she worked and saw nothing. Then, in the last room, she pulled the sheer curtains together and saw the girl in the reflection.

The scene was the same as before. A total massacre of blackened, twisted metal, an enormous blast scar toward the back of the old bus—she recognized it now—and her burnt dream daughter with her eyes and everything inside her skull removed. The image horrified Luisa. She crossed herself and looked away.

The sky rained soldiers. They fell from the floating tractor-trailer. As soon as they touched ground, one of them ran to the young girl's body. He dropped to his knees and hid his tears from the other men. His face was familiar, even through the grimace: the soldier who had helped Luisa and the girl get on the old bus. He took a vial from his pocket and popped off the lid, then poured a liquid over the charred body. She glowed bright green from head to toe, then crumpled to ash. Luisa crossed herself again. Her knees buckled and gave way. She fell to the floor and wailed.

The memories transfer injection went well. Ottaya remained groggy and couldn't recall much about the ordeal. She'd been attached to a mess of wires, while science team members spoke over one another and shined bright lights in her eyes. Even though a part of her father had been injected into her, she felt no closer to him than she had before. The disconnection made her sad, and melancholy followed her as she drifted off to sleep.

She remembered Vinto smiling down at her, telling her everything would be all right. Ottaya sensed him nearby. She forced her eyes open to the shadow of the air convoy above. She picked up on Vinto, but perceived nothing from her father's memories.

She would be happy to see the older woman again, but knew she needed rest before her arrival to help her get on the transport. Ottaya looked forward to the warmth of her body sitting next to her. The foreign woman comforted Ottaya and made her feel safe.

The next time she woke, they'd stopped at a checkpoint. Ottaya got off the bus and looked around. Relief coursed through her, and she smiled when she saw the older woman waiting at the side of the building. Ottaya neared, and the foreigner approached her with happiness. She opened her arms and wrapped them around Ottaya. Ottaya didn't understand the physical greeting. Then a look of dread came across the woman's face. As they walked back to the side of the building, the woman's incessant gibberish intensified. Ottaya stopped, placed her hands on the woman's shoulders, and in a calm, clear voice, told her everything would be all right. The foreigner relaxed, then reached into her bag and took out another one of those yellow things. Ottaya accepted and wolfed it down.

Once more, Vinto escorted them onto the transport. The old woman nudged Ottaya forward so she walked next to him.

"How long will it take to get to the lab?" Ottaya asked.

"Not long. Two moons." "Why not suns?"

"Suns, moons, same thing." Ottaya smiled at him.

"How are you feeling?" he said. "Good."

"Are you ready to end this?" "Endings also mean beginnings."

Vinto leaned over and kissed her cheek. Ottaya turned around.

The old woman had a big smile across her face.

Ottaya felt weak as soon as they sat in the transport.

Vinto loaded up into the air convoy after walking them to their seats. The old woman held Ottaya close as the transport moved on.

An explosion jarred Ottaya from sleep. Chaos had erupted on the transport. The old woman stood her upright, pushed her into the aisle, shoving her to the front. Frightened, Ottaya grabbed the rails. She got caught among others fleeing the transport. Deegan's throat had been slit; blood spray covered everything.

Forceful hands pushed her toward the door. The old woman was no longer behind her. Ottaya grabbed the handrail, dug her boots into the rubber padding on the floor and held her ground. The old woman struggled with Yorn. He held a blade and brought it down into her chest. Ottaya screamed. The old woman looked back, yelled at Ottaya, and then pulled something in Yorn's coat.

The tall man back shouted, "He's got mines!"

Everyone pushed in a wave. Ottaya lost her grip and flew out the doorway.

Luisa didn't trust the man in the back of the bus. She'd awakened before the crash and saw him kill the driver. She pretended to be asleep like everyone else. He hurried back to his seat and waited for the bus to hit something and cause a commotion. Luisa knew he wanted to hurt the young girl, take her eyes and brain. She couldn't let it happen. As soon as the bus crashed, Luisa got the girl up and pushed her into the moving crowd. Then ran to the back and tackled the man, hoping he'd hit his head and get knocked out. That didn't happen.

While Luisa fought him, she felt things under his coat. They reminded her of grenades she'd seen government forces use during her country's civil war. Then the man stabbed. Adrenaline pumped so hard through her body, the pain distant. Luisa thought of the young girl. She saw her and shouted, *"Te amo, mi hija."* and pulled a pin from one of the devices in the man's jacket. His eyes widened.

Luisa pulled him close, forcing the knife deeper into her chest. She held him with a strength she'd never known. Then all went silent before bright light swallowed—

Ottaya awoke on something soft but itchy green. She sat up and moved her palm across the tips and they tickled her skin. She rolled over and saw the old woman's carryall. Ottaya lay there, admiring a blue sky that was familiar, and yet . . . not quite. She wondered if it might be one of her father's memories. Tall buildings surrounded her, still intact and new: concrete flesh instead of steel and brick skeletons she'd been more accustomed to seeing.

Dark shadows took shape and descended from the clouds in a formation she recognized. Rebel air convoys filled the sky. Ottaya rose and ran with the old woman's bag clutched in her hands. She needed to find safety, and a lab where she could wait for the resistance, and Vinto—they would help her. The memories of her father would save this world.

DOWN BUT NOT OUT AT THE END OF THE WORLD

BY LISA MORTON

WHEN SANTIAGO WAKES IN THE HUMID PLASTIC tent it takes him a few seconds to identify what has intruded on his sleep. He lies there, sweating in his threadbare t-shirt and shorts, waiting, listening.

An engine. A car—big, maybe even a truck—approaches.

His stomach grumbles, and his hunger jolts him back to full awareness.

It's the same engine he's heard once a week for the last month. The one he hears just before another of his friends goes missing.

It's the only engine he's heard since everything fell apart. He's not sure when that happened, exactly—has it been months, years?—but it's when the traffic stopped, when the missions closed down. That hadn't been a big deal, really, because it was also when the cops stopped coming. With the cops gone, Santiago and his friends had begun scavenging downtown L.A.'s warehouses for food. In some ways it was better than it had been before. They knew something had happened— Santiago had heard vague stories about super-viruses and riots and famine—but for those already stripped of everything, nothing changed much.

As the engine sound nears, Santiago slips on shoes and pulls the tent flap open just enough to peer out.

It's a bright yellow Hummer, looks brand new, as if it just rolled out of a showroom that's been locked for months. It drives along slowly, the engine so strong that it makes the asphalt beneath Santiago thrum.

The first time it came, his friend Manny was gone the next day. The second time, it was a wiry young addict everyone called Pinto. The third time, it'd been Enoida. That one had hurt bad; he'd known Enoida for ten years, thought of her almost as a sister.

The thought of Enoida makes him burn, and the burning thrusts him to his feet and out of the tent. He knows there's probably nothing he can do, but he wants to know. He wants to know why his friends have vanished, he wants to know what will happen tonight. He wants to make something happen; he might be hungry and homeless, but at thirty-two he's still strong, in good shape, almost like he was when he came up from El Salvador eight years ago. During the hot days he works as a laborer, although he no longer works for money; now he works for the pleasure of helping others.

Santiago runs a few feet after the Hummer.

It slows. It stops.

Santiago's stomach lurches. Maybe this was a mistake.

It's night and the big car's windows are tinted so Santiago can't see in, but one rolls down, just a few inches. Something moves in the open space above the glass. The only light comes from the Hummer's headlights and a burning trash can on the street. By the time Santiago sees the glint of flames off a black barrel, it's too late. There's a loud *pop*, something stings in Santiago's neck. His hand instinctively moves up, finds something small and metal. He hears a male voice whoop.

His consciousness shuts down.

When Santiago's eyes open, he's no longer looking up at the inside of a cheap tent, and even the smoggy night sky is partially obscured by something. He recovers quickly and sits up as he tries to understand what's happened.

"*Buenos noches*," he hears a male voice say, the Spanish badly pronounced.

There are three men standing a few meters away, grouped around the parked Hummer. They're dressed in hunter chic—designer camouflage pants and jackets, t-shirts bearing the logos of gun companies and vanished corporations—but what really makes Santiago's stomach muscles clench are their guns. He knows now that he was shot by a tranquilizer gun, and although he doesn't know much about guns, he's fairly sure that what the three men hold now are hunting rifles, the kind stocked with bullets. The men grin at him; one bounces from foot to foot in excitement.

Santiago's eyes dart around, trying to fix his location. He sees flat, plain concrete around him, hears the slight trickle of water. He's in the L.A. River's lined channel; he guesses the structure overhead is the First Street bridge.

The men are saying something to him, but his panic turns the words into an incomprehensible stream of English. He's surprised to find he's not bound, so he rises slowly to his feet. He wonders why the men aren't shooting him yet. He hears "friends" and "meat" and "hunt," and his blood stops in his veins. One of the men burps, and Santiago knows what happened to his friends. In a world without fresh meat, these men have figured out a way to make their own.

One of them taps his watch and nods south along the channel. Santiago glances behind him, sees nothing.

The man screams, *"Now!"*

Santiago understands they want him to run.

He does.

Behind him, the men laugh. He wonders how long they'll wait before they fire, where the first bullet will hit, what it'll feel like. Mostly he runs.

In a few more meters he starts to think. Maybe he can still escape. They've brought him to the river channel because it's flat, open, they can run him down easily.

He has to get out of the channel. He abruptly swerves to his right, running for the embankment.

Behind him, he hears the men shout in alarm. A shot sounds. It strikes the concrete to the right of Santiago; a chip hits the exposed flesh of his right calf, but he doesn't stop. He makes it to the top of the channel, gets his bearings. Remembers where the surrounding fence is breached. It's not far. He runs, hoping the angle of the embankment makes him harder to hit.

He hears the Hummer's engine rev. They're coming.

Santiago's breath is fire in his lungs, he's gulping in air, but there's no slowing down. He finds the opening, a place where chain link has been clipped away to allow access to the River. He ducks through, is now on the train tracks that line the area next to the channel.

Another shot. Pain flares in Santiago's arm and an impact staggers him. He glances back, sees the men pressed against the fence, rifle barrels resting on wire. A look down shows him a bleeding gouge in his left arm where the bullet caught him. It's not serious; he's lucky.

He dodges as more shots sound. Santiago runs in shadow, hears them shout as the Hummer's engine sounds. The big vehicle will find its way down here in seconds. Ahead of him is a line of train cars. He cuts toward them, but realizes they'll expect him to hide out in there. He can't risk it. Although his heart is pounding and his leg muscles stretched to the snapping point, he tries to redouble his speed as he heads for the nearest building. It's an old office complex, empty.

He hears the Hummer coming as he enters the building. He knows he's leaving a trail of blood; his hunters will use it to track him down. His strength is flagging; it won't be long.

Unless...

Unless he can reach his "home", find his friends and rally them to help him. Hide him. Fight for him.

Even though the interior of this old building is in darkness, he remembers the layout enough to stumble his way through, avoiding one stairwell and an open elevator shaft. He's almost out the other side when he hears them. They're coming in where he did, following his blood. Santiago catches the gleam of flashlights. They'll be through soon.

He scrambles out the front. He's four blocks now from his tent and his friends. He runs along the empty street.

The Hummer squeals around a corner.

Santiago ducks into a building as it drives by, seeking him. He crouches down, holding his left arm, feeling the warm, thick blood pooling around his fingers.

When the Hummer passes by, Santiago dashes out and across the street, crouching, staying low. There's an old parking lot on the other side, weeds starting to reclaim the asphalt. He runs through the lot and continues on down the sidewalk. Behind him, on the other side of the street, his hunters leave the office building. He hears them pause, knows they're trying to find the red splotches that will reveal his direction.

He makes an intersection, goes right. He's slowing down now, but he doesn't have far to go. He risks a pause to catch his breath, but when he hears his pursuers, adrenaline jolts him into motion again. He's half-jogging half-stumbling, he can't go much longer . . .

A figure appears before him.

Santiago pulls up short, expecting the shot that will end his life—but then a sour smell hits him, and he realizes the man before him is Billy, an old junkie whose last bath was in an earlier decade. Santiago husks out, "*¡Carrera!*" He dodges around Billy, praying the old man vanishes.

Santiago hears several rifle pops when he reaches the next intersection. He knows Billy is dead. He hears the hunters exclaim in disgust when they reach the corpse.

They're still coming.

Another block, and he sees the orange firelight ahead. Not far now . . .

Is he doing the right thing? Will they decide to kill more of his friends? Should he stop now, let them take him to spare the others?

No. If they take him, put a bullet through his heart, cart the body back to their well-fed families, they'll just be back again. Maybe it won't be a month between visits; maybe it'll be a week, then a day. Maybe more of them will come soon, more of their kind who are hungry for something fresh.

No. He can't let that happen. Not to *his* people.

Santiago is half a block now. The tent on the corner houses Wash, a kid with skin the color of night and hands the size of Santiago's head. If anyone can help, it's Wash. Santiago begins shouting, his voice hoarse. He just makes sounds, not bothering to form words.

He's almost to the start of the tent city when the Hummer's engine approaches. Tires squeal as it rounds a corner. It's there, in front of Santiago. His strength fails; he can't run any more. He stands, waiting, numb, as the driver's door opens and one of the hunters climbs out, grabbing his rifle. He raises it, slowly. As he finally sights down the barrel, he calls out, "C'mon, run, ya fuckin' loser. Give me a little sport, will ya?"

Santiago doesn't move.

The hunter murmurs, "Fuck you, then."

Santiago tenses, awaiting his murder—

The rifleman drops. Wash stands behind him with an iron pipe clenched in one fist.

Wash doesn't speak much Spanish, so Santiago puts his exhaustion aside to dredge up the English. "Two more coming!"

Wash looks around, sees the open driver's door of the Hummer. He gets in, closes the door, guns the engine.

"Hey—!"

Santiago spins. The two others are behind him, coming, raising their rifles.

The Hummer leaps forward, burning rubber as it curves around Santiago and heads for the hunters. One of them raises his rifle and tries to shoot Wash through the front windshield, but his bullet only cracks the safety glass before the huge vehicle plows over him. His friend dives to the side, rolling.

The Hummer tries to pull a high-speed U-turn but it spins too far, 360 degrees before stopping. As Wash grinds the gears and tries to get the Hummer turned around, the last hunter reaches his knees, raises the rifle, and sights on Santiago.

That's when an upended trash can comes down on him, knocking the rifle aside, driving him to the pavement. An elderly woman known only as Mama is behind the hunter, breathing heavy from having lifted the heavy can. The hunter tries to rise, but three others join Mama, they carry two-by-fours and lengths of metal rebar, and they descend on the hunter.

It's over. Santiago has won.

But it's not enough. As Wash pulls the Hummer up next to him, Santiago picks up one of the rifles. He experiments with it, feeling its weight, working the bolt action, firing off a test round. It is, of course, an expensive piece of equipment, the best.

Santiago walks around the Hummer, opens the passenger door, reaches into the glove compartment, finds the registration. There's an address on it. Santiago tosses it to Wash. "Can you find this?"

Wash scans the registration and nods. "Yeah. Yeah, I can find it."

Santiago looks around. Dozens of the people from the tent city are watching. Wash waves them forward. They fill up the rear of the Hummer, while Wash and Santiago take the front seats, both armed with the rich men's guns. They'll take the fight to their foes now.

Santiago can't help but wonder if they shouldn't have done this long ago.

THE RUINERS

BY JOHN PALISANO

THERE IS NOTHING BUT TIME LEFT TO THINK, EVEN as time seems to be slipping away. Before the snow drifts turned to small glaciers, winter was welcome. The cold air once refreshed and inspired me. Now it's my enemy.

At first glimpse I swore what I saw poking out of the water onto the ice-covered beach was just a piece of driftwood. Was I just seeing things?

It moved a bit, then stopped, and I resumed prepping my daily test of the water's chemical content, a job I'd taken after the paper closed, and a friend at the college offered it to me in exchange of a cinder block-walled dorm room just off campus.

I had been alone, standing near the place where the runoff and Manhattan Beach pier connect, dropping in the Mercer test monitor, scanning the water, just like I did every other day. The rich athletes and movie producers had long ago left the coasts for places over the mountains. Before the freeze they paid for the cool ocean breezes giving them moderate temperatures while the rest of Southern California roasted. Those days seemed made up. The ocean breezes made the newly cool world even more unbearable. I'd stuck around, my work as a reporter fallen away, but the water-testing job kept me off the street. I couldn't believe I'd been reduced to such a life. I have Robin ... my ex-wife ... to thank for that new normal, don't I? At least our son didn't mind. He dug visiting me at the college. Saw it as an adventure.

The rectangular machine bubbled inside the water just a bit; I saw it between two plates of ice. I held its tether and watched all the lights turn yellow. When they turned blue it'd be finished. The entire process only took a few minutes.

From the corner of my eye I saw the piece of driftwood rise up and out as if it were a sword someone was cutting through with.

When it moved upward my first thought was there was a strong tide and maybe a storm breaking.

Quite quickly I could tell what I was witnessing was not driftwood at all, but, rather, some kind of sea beast rising from the water, breaking through slabs of ice.

Once the rest of the creature's leg slipped up and out of the freezing Pacific Ocean, though, I knew we had trouble. It was no longer our world. We'd finally lost control. The ice had signaled a change no one's darkest dreams could have predicted. No one more than me wished the world still had more than winter as a season.

The Mercer testing unit's lights went all blue. *Good timing*, I thought. *Damn thing.* I pulled it from the water and slung it over my shoulder. Whatever data it collected was already transmitted back to the school.

The thing was up and out of the water in a blink. It looked similar to a spider or crab at first, only two stories tall. It looked around, scanning the frozen landscape around it from its group of seven eyes. A hundred half-remembered comic-book creatures came up, my head trying to catalog and name the beast.

I stopped dead. I wanted to run. Hide. Be anywhere else. My heart felt like it stalled and raced at the same time. My throat tightened.

Use that training. Tae Kwon Do. Control your head and tame your thoughts. Isolate the fear. Use the adrenaline like fuel. Don't let it rule you. Come on. You can. That's how you'll survive.

I thought back to growing up. It flashed in a blink. Guess it was my mind trying to make sense of things and to try and figure out a way to survive. My mom took me to the beach almost every day of every summer until I was a teenager. I knew the place inside out, even with the heavy layer of snow and ice hiding most of it. There were still landmarks. Yes. Landmarks. That was it. The lifeguard house. That'd be a good place to hide out. Hopefully.

Could I make it?

Yes. But the thing might see me. So then what? Could it get inside?

Likely. Very likely.

I'd be running into my grave.

There had to be somewhere else.

While I was standing there with my metaphoric finger on my metaphoric lip, wondering, the huge sea creature advanced toward me.

Trust your instincts. Come on.

I hurried through the snow-covered beach.

Clunk. Clunk. Clunk. My steps sunk deep as my feet crunched through the hard top layer. I moved slowly . . . much too slowly. It was going to catch me and eat me before I'd ever get a chance to hide.

Hunkering down to lower my profile, I imagined doing so may have helped hide me. *You're a black man, dressed in black, running through snow. What do you think?*

So I just hurried, not daring to look backward and see the thing coming. If I saw it, and if the beast made eye contact with me, that'd be the end. They'd lock in. Maybe I was just so much debris running away. Not that I saw anything else.

The two minutes it took for me to cross the beach felt like two hours. I was sure the creatures were going to get me at any turn.

Behind me I sensed the creature was several large steps away from the pier. There may have been a place to hide when there was low tide, but with the high water and the snow and ice? I figured I was a goner.

It was right up on me.

Playground.

There were these weird sculptures they'd put in for us kids to climb when I was in second grade.

I don't believe you. I don't believe a word you say.

That was Joanna's voice in my head, left over from middle school. She never believed me. If we would've been older, it would have been a joke. But seeing as we were both thirteen, it stuck with me. It didn't matter what I said or did, she'd always tell me, and everyone else within earshot, how full of crap she thought I was. She especially relished it if I raised my hand to answer a question in class and got it wrong. She'd whisper "See?" and the teacher would tell her, "That's enough." My friends told me she probably liked me. My mom told me the same thing. I guess we were just too young to figure that out. I always thought she was beautiful, but she ruined my ever liking her. Even if I'd made moves, I'm sure she wasn't of mind to act on it, either. Her words stuck with me throughout my life. For some reason, I always wanted her to believe me.

Don't

Believe

A

Word

Would she believe me if she saw the huge creature lifting itself out of the water? Would she still be telling everyone what a liar I was?

I heard Robin's voice in my head. *It's over now. I'm sorry. We had a good run.*

So much for "in sickness and in health". Wedding vows meant nothing. I still didn't want to believe in such a profound betrayal. All these years later. Sometimes I still woke up and believed we were together again. It seemed so real. I could smell our old bedroom: the lavender sheets, the vanilla candles, her breath. Finding myself alone in a cold dorm room, instead, was jarring. The mind is tricky. It can play your deepest desires on your inner theatre and fool you into thinking they're real.

All that went through my head. All that in a blink. The adrenaline raced in my head, too. My brain was like a supercomputer scanning a film a thousand feet and scenes a second... processing... thinking... searching for an answer to this:

What the hell do I do?

Hide, idiot. Take shelter. Find somewhere safe, then think about what to do next.

Right.

I did.

The lifeguard house was only a short jump away from me. *No key. Probably locked tight.*

So what. At least it can be some kind of shelter. A wall, if nothing else.

I made it in a blink. From the corner of my eye I saw the thing lifting even higher from the water. It was huge ... as large as a tree ... at least ... and its limbs looked like those of an alien crustacean. They were colored in reflected blues, greens, and yellows reminding me of the type you'd see in oil if you looked to the side.

At the lifeguard house, which was little more than a cottage they used to triage beachgoers, have breaks, and change, I'd been right it'd been locked up. Not only locked, but they'd secured the heavy metal screen doors for the winter ... the brutal, punishing winter we'd had been going through that never seemed to end.

Making my way toward the back of the lifeguard house, I spotted a second large beast rising from the water. The first beast had made it onto the snow-covered beach, the sword-like ends of its appendages crashing through the ice and into the sand beneath, sending small explosions of the beach on top of the snow. They looked like huge crabs on the bottom, but something entirely different on top. They were soft up there—a rubber, moving bit with moving black cable-like things slithering through the air.

What the hell?

The beast lumbered forward.

I was glad to make it to the back of the house so I couldn't see the beasts. If they'd seen me, I had a feeling they'd be able to make quick work of the lifeguard house, anyway. They were massive and huge.

Hope they can't sense me. Smell me. See me. Feel me. Who knows?

The windows on back were not covered with metal grates like the doors, but with white-painted pieces of wood. I could likely get through them, but could I fit through? I evaluated the size and knew I could. First I'd need to get myself up a little higher. There was nothing around.

Robin in my head again. *I just don't believe in us anymore. I don't think we have a future. I don't believe in you. You just don't have your life together. You always let me down.*

My voice, from so long ago. *I do. I think we're just getting started. The best is yet to come. I know if you stick with me it'll be worth it. It's just a bumpy patch. I believe in us.*

Her. *It's more than that. Much more. I don't believe in us anymore. I don't believe in you. I don't think you'll ever add up to anything.*

The beach shook.

The beasts were coming, stomping into the ground.

Another trembler nearly knocked me off my feet. I was surprised to realize I'd still kept my test kit. I hadn't even thought to drop it when I'd hurried toward the lifeguard house.

Robin's voice haunted me, playing over and over in a maddening loop. *I don't believe in you . . . don't think . . . you'll add up . . . to anything . . . ever.*

Don't
Believe
A
Word

My insides went cold. I was sick. Just like all the others. Whatever phenomena causing the globe's temperatures to plummet and bathe the world in thick drifts of white snow had also caused severe problems with all its living beings. Many succumbed to everlasting flu and pneumonia, while others had no outward physical symptoms, but suffered dementia or hallucinations or incurable madness.

No. Not hallucinations. Face this, man. Rise up. Don't back down. Keep your head.

Destroyers. Conquerors. Ruiners. Yes. They ruined everything we had. That had to be what the things were. They looked like every science-fiction and horror-movie monster I'd ever seen, wrapped together in a hellish conglomerate.

The things came for me.

Don't
Believe
A
Thing
Not

A
Damn
Thing
You
See

I shut my eyes and I could still hear them lumbering around, but then I pictured them not, and they soon silenced. My monsters faded nearly as quickly as they'd come.

Peeking around the side of the lifeguard house, I saw the beach back to how it'd been. Blankets of ash-like snow covered the sand. The surface appeared bumpy and uneven. Could they hide the footprints of the beasts? Maybe one was on top of the lifeguard house, figuring out if it did and remained silent, it'd gain unquestionable advantage.

Don't move.

It had to have been above me. That was the only explanation.

I looked around to see if there were any signs.

Robin's voice chimed in. *You mess everything up. You always make bad choices.*

I talked back to her. *No I didn't. Another word for mistakes is learning. For finding your way.*

Find your way.

Now!

I took a deep breath. Water dripped from the lip of the roof.

The snow was melting, but just a little bit. It'd all refreeze once the night came.

Slowly, I leaned my head out and looked up.

No sign of the beast.

Stepping away from the guardhouse, it became obvious quickly the only thing on the roof was a pile of frozen-over snow.

Scanning the beach, I looked for signs of the beasts.

Nothing.

Where had they gone?

Maybe back underwater, and back within the depths from where they came. Like a bad daydream wiped away.

They were here just a few minutes ago. They were so real. Maybe they just went somewhere else. Maybe they flew away.

I looked out at the frozen landscape. That was what the world had become. That was my new reality. Life had changed forever, whether I was on board or not.

My head. My blessed, cursed, sick head. Was something wrong? Had I finally caught the bug and hallucinated? Maybe I was in a hospital bed somewhere and everything wasn't real.

No. The cold was too present.

I stood where I stood, existed where I existed.

The Mercer testing unit beeped. I looked down and saw the lights had all turned orange. It'd sent along its message back to the college.

I looked out toward the town and saw the beasts. They hadn't gone back inside the ocean, they'd gone searching for better things to ruin.

They towered over the town, moving gracefully and elegantly.

They're looking for people like they were looking for me. What are they going to do once they find people? Are they going to move on, like they did with me? Or are they going to stop and crack skulls and kill and lay waste to everything, taking our world for their own?

The punishing snow started up again. The endless winter cycled, burying what we'd built while unleashing these things that had been waiting for only God knows how long. I wondered where the Ruiners had come from. Were they ancient creatures who'd been asleep under the water since time immortal? Were they aliens that had crashed, only able to surface once the temperature of the planet had plunged low enough to sustain them and weaken us? Did it really matter? Were they tied to the cold pulses? Had to be.

Why did it pass you by? Why didn't it take you?

I wasn't sure, but I had a feeling there was something to that. Maybe it'd been the Mercer unit? Maybe it was something in me? Was it because I was black? Something that stood out against the blanket of whiteness? There had to be something.

Finding out was my destiny. Of that I was never more sure.

I took one last look at the landscape in back of me—looked at the huge blocks of ice moving ever so slightly on the ocean—and started the long, cold trip toward the college.

The cold and the loneliness may never end, but I'm not going to let the Ruiners take what little we have left.

I was a thing she didn't believe in. I'd change her mind. I'd prove to her I was worth it. I'd just have to pull off figuring out the Ruiners and then finding her. That was the trick.

You're a scientist. Your mind is spectacular. Always has been. You can figure this out. The answers are there. You simply need to find them. And you can find Robin, too. You know her well, and know where she'd go. This is what you were made for.

There was a massive, thunderous sound coming from where the Ruiners had gone. They'd made work of a small gas station, tearing the roof from above the pumps and throwing it into the street adjacent.

This is like watching those giant monster movies as a kid. But it's real. Can't be. That stuff was all make-believe. Come on.

But it is.

Anything is possible.

See it as a scientist.

Of course it's possible.

And it's possible to fix it.

Could I do so alone?

You just said it, buddy, didn't you?

Anything is possible.

Slogging my way back up the hill toward the main part of town, the wind kicked in and froze my face. I had a memory of the first day the deep cold came.

The school bell had just rung. The kids at Sand Beach Elementary were filing out. Some were talking smack to one another near me, in the playful, harmless way kids do—the stuff that seemed to be life-threatening back then. You know: you like a show and another kid says they don't, and it feels like a personal insult to end them all. But we grow up and we mature. We would deal with real issues as grown-up life crept in.

Most of those kids wouldn't know.

Everything shook a bit.

"It's an earthquake!" one yelled.

"What do we do when we're outside?" another said.

All this in a blink. My thoughts went into overdrive. My boy. My son. Eric. Find him.

I called for Eric. In a remarkable bit of luck, he'd taken a different route and had run out to surprise me. He tugged on the back of my shirt. "Dad?"

I'd never been more relieved. "Kiddo," I said. "Thank God." I grabbed the crook of his arm and led him toward the gate and the street nearby where I parked the 4Runner. "Let's get home."

"Okay."

We made it to the curb and waited with a crowd of other kids and a few parents. The crossing guard blew his whistle for everybody to stop. We did.

Cars inched forward. There was a massive rumbling sound. I looked for the garbage truck or semi, which it had to be, then thought how they weren't allowed on Aliso Canyon Road, where we were.

Wasn't a truck.

Another quake.

Something inside me knew it wasn't a quake, either. But what? The earth hadn't rolled or shook. It was over and I shrugged it off.

Our 4Runner was only a half a block away. We could see it. Finally, the crossing guard guy blew the whistle and we got to go across the street. "I can't wait for our weekend," Eric said. "Maybe we can go to Six Flags?"

"Maybe," I'd said, instantly trying to think of something else we could do.

We got to the 4Runner and I clicked my keychain to unlock the doors. Eric climbed in. I got in. I checked to see his seatbelt was on.

He'd already done it. He turned to me and smiled. "Thank God that's over," he said. He waved at a pretty girl with long, straight brown hair. "Bye, Sophie," he said.

She waved back.

Her face dropped.

She wrapped her arms around herself. Her teeth chattered.

The world changed in a moment.

"Is she okay?" I asked.

"I don't know," Eric said. "Sophie?" She couldn't hear either of us.

The big, rumbling sound came again, only louder, like a million hell hounds cheering on the end of the world.

Everything froze as the cold blast slammed us.

Sophie fell to her knees. We saw the other kids get knocked down as well. I looked in the rearview mirror and saw the crossing guard flat on his back, his stop sign fallen on the road beside him.

No one was left standing.

The front window of the 4Runner looked blurry and I realized it'd frozen over.

Wind howled.

Snow flurries fell.

"What just happened?" Eric asked. "Dad?"

"I don't know," I said. My thoughts turned to causes. Could it be nuclear winter from an A-bomb? What could cause a cold blast like that? We lived in Southern California, not Antarctica. It made no sense. Was everyone dead? "Stay in the car. I don't know what the hell is going on."

"Sophie," he said. "She's not moving." I turned and saw he was right. A light dusting of snow had already covered her.

"Don't look," I said.

"Is she going to be okay?" he asked.

Before I could respond, cold air breached the cabin of the 4Runner. I'd never felt anything like it on the West Coast. Eric immediately shook. "Dad," he said. "It's cold."

I turned and grabbed a few blankets we'd used for camping. "Here." I wrapped him and noticed my own hands were shaking.

Start the car.

I knew we had to get out of there. We were in the middle of something deadly serious.

Please start.

I turned the key.

The familiar sound of the engine made me gasp.

"Oh, thank God," I said, hoping the rest of the mechanicals would function. I put it in first gear and we rolled forward. "We have to find Mom," he said.

"Right," I said.

We drove onto Flower Road, past the few dozen children and occasional adult frozen to the sidewalks and street.

The whole thing reminded me of the figures they unearthed from Pompeii, frozen in time, curled into fetal positions as the volcano's fumes blasted the air from their lungs.

That had been a lot like what had happened that afternoon to us, only it wasn't super-heated air, it was super-cooled.

The neighborhood just past the school was void of people. It usually was, which was lucky for us. We didn't need to see any more dead.

The heater in the 4Runner worked.

"I can't believe there's snow everywhere," Eric said. "This is crazy."

"We don't know what it is," I said. "It may be something toxic."

"Like from the Porter Ranch gas leak?"

"Something like that," I said. "Sure. I'm trying to think."

"You're a scientist," he said. "You're smart. I'm sure you'll figure it out."

"I'm not so sure," I said. "This is unprecedented."

"What does that mean?"

"It's never happened before."

The mountain vistas normally looking like powdered cocoa were all covered in snow. During the winter, that wasn't so unusual. Only thing was there was a lot more of it than the snow-capped ridges we'd grown used to.

"Do you think if I close my eyes all of this will go away?" Eric asked.

"I wish it were that easy," I said. We made our way to his mom's house.

My mind was busy computing what the probability was for different scenarios that could have caused the cold blast. I wish like hell I would have been paying more attention to Eric, but how was I to know what was coming next?

When we got to his mom's house, it looked deserted. "Let me try my door first," I said. "Make sure it's safe."

I went to open my door but it stuck. The cold had frozen it to the frame. "Shoot," I said. It budged when I gave it a good shove with my shoulder. I wondered if that'd been a good idea. Say the cold blast was still coming? I'd kill us both.

Luckily it wasn't. Freezing air came inside the cab of the truck, but it didn't freeze our lungs and take us out.

I had a vision of all those kids frozen to the sidewalk—their backpacks frozen a few feet from them. It could have been Eric. If I'd been late, if we'd even lingered for a moment too long, we would have been dead, too. *Try not to think about it, man. You got lucky. Thank God you got lucky. Again.*

When I got out of the cab of the 4Runner I waved to Eric to stay put. I went up to Robin's door and knocked. She answered, rather quickly. She was wearing a robe over her clothes.

"I have Eric," I said. "I picked him up. This thing has happened . . . "

"I know," Robin said. "Where is he?"

"In the truck. I wanted to make sure you were here and everything was okay," I said.

She nodded, but something wasn't right with the way she looked. From the corner of my eye I saw a mound on the front lawn. A hand was visible stretching out from one side.

"Oh my God," I said. "Alan?"

"No," she said. "Thank God. It's our friend Bill. He was working on the fence." It was always *our friend*, implying, not yours, we have a life and you don't. She was such a shitty and spiteful human being.

"Shit," I said. "I'm sorry." I can't say I wasn't a little disappointed the man that replaced me wasn't dead. Damn it. That would have been just.

"He's fine. He's at work. He called."

"Your phone's working?" I asked.

"Everything's working," she said.

Now that I look back I'm not entirely sure she was being honest. Most of the city... most of the planet... had lost power. There were still pockets of utilities working, but not many.

I went to the cab and walked Eric to his mom.

"See you later, Dad," he said.

"Until next time," I said.

We had a thing where we didn't say goodbye, because it wasn't a goodbye forever.

"Remember to aim for the soft spots," he said and winked.

I laughed. That was something we'd always said to one another. It was in reference to something he'd heard in karate. When he'd asked me later what that meant, and I told him to use his imagination, well, it spurred tons and tons of laughter.

"You bet," I said, and turned before my emotions got the best of me. I hated dropping him off at his mom's more than anything. It felt unnatural and awful. Families should be together, not split apart.

Then I was gone.

We kept in contact through texts for a few days, and then those stopped.

There was another cold blast a couple of days after and I hoped like hell they were all inside and okay. I had no way of knowing.

My 4Runner stopped working. There must have been something in the latest blast that had destroyed it. That meant driving up to check on Eric was a no-go. I'd have to wait it out until things warmed a bit, or I figured out another way.

The Ruiners stopped their march halfway up the hill. They had brought their faces down into the snow.

I crept alongside the buildings to the west side of the street, where there was an overhang and fencing. Enough, I hoped, to camouflage me.

One put its long proboscis into the snow.

I knew what they were doing before it was obvious. There was a foot sticking from the mound of snow right where the Ruiner stood.

Its head moved slightly as it sucked the essence from the buried person.

My guts tightened.

Why hadn't they gone for me?

I had an idea. They were drawn to the bodies that had been flash frozen. Maybe that's how they preferred their meals. Freezing changes biological matter. Ice crystals can form. There can be massive damage. Similar to freezer burn on ice cream. I pictured it happening inside a human body. Blood would expand. Organs, too. Who knew why they preferred that to a live person?

Maybe they're like us. We don't exactly like to go out and kill cows to eat a cheeseburger. Maybe this is like that somehow.

One of the Ruiners found me.

For a moment I thought it would pass like the other.

It didn't.

It swung an arm at me, trying to get to me.

Shit!

I ducked and looked for a safe place to run, but I was trapped. My effort to hide had trapped me inside. There was a Ruiner on both sides of the walkway and one right in front.

They made horrible noises, screaming as if they were being boiled alive.

I was no match.

The one in front hit me with such a force, and so quickly, I was dropped on my ass in a blink. The Mercer testing unit went long.

Crap.

Now what.

It had inched up and over the small fence, pushing a garbage can out of the way to get to me.

The Ruiner's alien face appeared inches from my own.

I'm going to die.

Its black eyes stared into my own.

I felt it pushing me down. I was so cold I barely felt my body. A lot of that was the adrenaline, too, I'm sure.

Aim for the soft spots.

Eric's voice in my head.

Eric.

Only a few miles away.

I punched at the Ruiner's eyes with all I had.

I connected.

The creature screeched and backed out, batting at its eye.

Was that all it would take? One hit? Couldn't be. Wouldn't be that easy.

Something grabbed me around my middle and dragged me. Another Ruiner. *Now you've gone and done it, you idiot.*

I tried to grab something to stop the beast, but it was useless. It was too fast and strong and I was too weak.

Exposed again, I felt the thing's arm wrapped around my middle.

It lifted me. My stomach flipped. It was like an amusement park ride when you're shot up real fast and your body just reacts.

We towered up and over the town. I towered over the town.

Then it brought me backward.

Oh, no. This isn't going to . . .

The Ruiner flung me. Once it let me go I flew for a moment before I fell. I was sure I was going to die. Again. And they were going to drink me up after I splattered.

Maybe I was a cat in a past life. Nine lives and all. How many did I use up that morning? Six? Seven? Because when I hit the ground, the snow around me caved in and I found myself falling again.

I couldn't breathe but I couldn't believe I hadn't hit pavement. What had I hit?

I wasn't sure, but I froze as the snow cradled me.

As soon as I could I made work of trying to get out. My hand touched something—another person. Dead. I crawled my way upward. My feet touched the other person. I wanted to yell, but I was losing air. The weight of the snow around me was increasing. How? Maybe it'd been melting a bit, I wasn't sure. Maybe my fall had triggered more of it in a mini-avalanche.

With a few pulls, I had my head and torso out.

I spotted a diving board several feet away, covered in about two feet of snow, of course.

Holy shit had I been lucky. I'd fallen into a pool filled with snow.

Behind me I could see the dark outline of the person I'd been climbing away from. He wasn't the only one. There were dozens. All of their faces had lost their natural color and were grey and dark and sunken in, like mummies from hell.

I got out of there.

On the side of the pool I scanned the area. There were walls on each side. I inched my way toward one area where there was an exit. I saw nothing but white.

Then the snow began again.

Great timing, I thought. This will only make things worse.

But would it?

A storm would maybe be the best cover I would get.

I caught my breath. Before the world turned off there were several theories about the cold blast. Most centered on a short failure of our atmosphere. A hole, like in the ozone layer, had let in freezing cold space. It would have only taken a moment to do so. That would be why the world was frozen, but still there.

I tried to wrap my scientific brain around that theory, but it seemed implausible. How would it open and then close again? It would have had to have been a significantly large hole for that effect. Would outer space really leak inside? Or would our atmosphere simply just leak out? So many questions. Without any way of communicating or examining the world, the best I could do was to monitor the ocean close to me. It may have given us clues. I had come to the conclusion the Ruiners had to have something to do with the frozen earth. In fact, I was convinced they had everything to do with it. Maybe they weren't creatures that'd hibernated in the sea for ages. Maybe they'd come from outside, crashing through our atmosphere and letting the cold in.

As I made my way out from the pool area, I looked out and saw the three Ruiners. They were hundreds of feet away. There were dark spots all over the place—the bodies of people they'd already tapped.

A hand tapped my shoulder. I nearly screamed.

"Shush," said a voice. I turned and saw a fellow with a dark iced-over beard. "Come on."

He rushed toward the pool, back where I'd come from. It felt counterintuitive, but I knew if he'd made it this long, there was likely shelter somewhere close.

I was right. He led me into a small passage. "Walk slow," he said. "Don't make a lot of noise."

My body hurt. Everything hurt. What'd I'd just been through was starting to catch up to me. Big time.

"I'm Eli," he said.

Then we were inside a much larger room. There were people huddled on cots. There was a dim light from candles. People murmured. Some looked at me.

Then I recognized an orange pullover. It was one my wife Robin . . . I mean my ex-wife Robin . . . had worn for years. She turned. Eric was in back of her. He saw me and pointed, his eyes wide and full. "Dad!"

He ran to me and I never felt anything better in my whole life.

"How did you find us?" he asked.

"You know me," I said. "It's never goodbye. Just see you next time. And we were due for our next time."

"I always believed you'd come again for me, Dad," he said. "I always believed."

"Me, too," I said. "Me, too, kiddo."

And then I held my son for what felt like forever and the world thawed just a little bit, right then and there.

LAST NIGHT . . .

BY ERIC J. GUIGNARD

LAST NIGHT, THE MOON TURNED FULL.

Last night, the world stopped turning.

Last night, the cosmos froze, like the slow-moving cogs of an ancient clock that finally grind down. Perhaps the great horologist of the universe simply forgot to rewind the mechanism of its gears. Perhaps he will appear at any moment to lift the stop lever and turn back its counter wheel. Perhaps he has decided the clock is broken and not worth his patience to tinker with any longer.

The earth hangs motionless now, peering to the sun from one face which, presumably, must begin to burn. Is the other side of the planet in flames or is it simply cooking like a slow-roast oven? I cower in North Vancouver, across the Burrard Inlet and, here, it is only night. My own watch has outlasted the mechanism of the universe and ticks away, telling me it's three in the afternoon. The sky shows otherwise, black and interrupted by a soft moon which rests high above like a pool of cream.

The temperature had fortunately been warm, golden months of Canadian summer that were just beginning to fade into autumn's auburn embrace. But I feel it cooling already. The red mercury on my thermometer outdoors drops steadily—forty-eight degrees and slowly sinking. The electricity is still on to generate heat but, once that goes out, there will remain nothing to warm this part of land relegated to nocturnal shadows. Lest that great horologist return, I can only image the arctic wasteland all of Vancouver will soon become.

If the sinking cold were not grim enough, the howl of werewolves chills me even more.

It's true they exist, but they've been of little consequence. One night a month, they transformed and ran wild through the piney wilderness above Lion's Bay. Their victims were homeless vagrants found sleeping in ravines or drunken hunters, piss-proud they killed a rabbit with a shotgun. Poetic justice, if you ask me, and their deaths unmourned. We all knew of the creatures and simply stayed home those nights with doors locked and shutters bolted. The werewolves were people of the town, members of families with long-standing roots to the indigenous men and women who first settled this country. When the time of month came, they did their business elsewhere, and we let them be.

Now, however, the moon does not fall. It no longer cycles the earth, while the earth no longer cycles the sun. That beguiling orb in the sky has petrified and casts its strange call permanently over mortals who would transform into howling beasts: those mortals who will never be mortal again. As the cosmos are stuck in their current alignment, so too are the creatures stuck in their transformation. The moon may stay full on this part of land for the remainder of eternity, and the wolf-men will run wild.

Last week, the moon turned full.

Last week, the world stopped turning.

Last week, time fell meaningless as calculations based on the rotation of the planet ceased. My watch ticks onward, the quartz crystal in its center vibrating at a steady frequency to tell me the hours, the days that have passed. It matters not for, outside, it is still midnight... always midnight.

I look out the window and see the dark ocean far away, its surface illuminated by the moon's reflection. Burrard Inlet is motionless, flat as a sheet of glass. There are no tides to pull the waves in or out, motions I once let myself be hypnotized by, dreaming upon their quiet, steady roar. Little moves outside, except for glimpses of fleeting shadows that dart across the hills—shadows that quickly melt into darkness and, once they are gone, cause me to wonder if they were ever there to begin with.

The werewolves have grown bold. In the past they relegated themselves to the wilderness, but now they roam the city. Their number is multiplying. I hear howling often, and screams too, but can never tell where the sound comes from as it echoes in the cold, still night air.

I have gone outside my house only twice since the world stopped moving.

The first time, I sought my neighbors to exclaim the wonder, the terror of what occurred. I am old and lonely and fear, most of all, enduring the end of life by myself. I thought unity, companionship was crucial for us all—the catastrophe of what occurred too great for anyone to bear alone.

Those I visited, however, were already touched by hopelessness, searching in their own ways for acceptance of the event.

I visited the cottage across the road first. Mrs. Gordon sobbed when she saw me, and her voice choked when she spoke. "My marigolds will die."

I embraced her and said I would replant them next season.

She smiled and nodded. She wore a pink bathrobe with images of angels playing lutes, and she wiped her nose on its sleeve.

"Thank you," she said. "Perhaps you may come back tomorrow when I prune the daffodils."

"I will," I quietly replied.

The next house down the road was Jim Franklin's. He sat on a rocker on his porch, swaying back and forth in a parka. He stared at the moon with a shotgun on his lap.

"The Mayans were right," he told me.

"I think we should band together, share resources," I said.

"What's the point?"

I couldn't answer. He kept swaying, and I left.

I went to other houses as well, knocking on doors while nervously looking over my shoulder. Families were either missing or they chased me away with curses and guns. I have always believed the full moon has a strange effect on people, whether they're werewolves or not.

I returned home, and later that night the electricity went out. Most of the older homes out here have backup generators, as do I, and I know to use it sparingly. Everything is turned off, except for the heater. Outdoors, it is nineteen degrees and so cold.

Sometime later I went outside again, my second time, to check on the neighbors.

Mrs. Gordon was gone. The door to her house hung open, and her marigolds were torn up and flung across the yard, as if a wild animal dug in her garden.

At Jim Franklin's house, I found him lying in the yard on his back.

"Jim, are you okay?" I whispered.

He lay naked and mauled. Fresh wounds channeled across his chest and arms, and torn strips of flesh revealed imprints of teeth marks. His skin shone mottled blue-grey from the frost, though patches of fur began to push through. He convulsed with transformation, and veins bulged as if rope coiled under his skin. At sight of me, he growled deeply and slowly rose.

Across the road, I caught glimpse of a great beast dart between trees. It stood upright and was covered in dark hair. In that moment I saw the beast's eyes glow like sparks of fire and, I saw too, it wore a tattered pink bathrobe.

I fled home and barricaded myself inside.

My house could be considered cozy and safe, a historic marker, dating to the late nineteenth century, built of thick stone and brick. The windows are glass though, and that worries me. I've moved furniture and nailed planks across the panes, but for how long it will last, I don't know. Not much longer, I suppose, and then I will retreat to the wine cellar beneath the floor. I mostly stay down there anyway, bundled in bedding and thick coats.

I listen to the ticks of my watch counting away moments that have no meaning and wonder at the world. I think of the small stockpile of food and water down in the cellar and wonder how long it will last. I wonder how I will die.

I have a prescription bottle of sleeping pills, should I decide to end this nightmare on my own terms. I wonder if there is someone left who will judge me on the choices I make.

Last month, the moon turned full.

Last month, the world stopped turning.

Last month, the human race began to die. Whether by climate-induced chaos or the wolf creatures' advance, I have seen nor heard anything evidencing mankind as I once defined it. Day-by-day the lights of mankind extinguished. The sky turned dark and then, for me, darker still.

I long for the moonlight now, as I cower in the shelter of the wine cellar. Down here, it is black as the shadows of dreams and cold as the realization I will never wake from them. When I leave my bedding, I crawl blindly on hands and knees to feel for the shrinking stockpile of food. I shiver as much from terror as from the cold. The werewolves are above me, and they smell my fear down here. They bang on the iron door overhead and howl in frustration, vicious snarls that slash at me almost as painfully as their claws surely would.

As I suspected, they came in through the windows. Three of them broke through, baying in unison, and leapt at me. One of the creatures was missing its left ear, and I think now of Max Everman who ran the Shell gas station and had his ear blown off in a hunting accident back in '87.

When the werewolves attacked I escaped, barely, into the cellar, screaming like a child. An hour later, the generator went out. That occurred several days ago.

I don't know how cold it is, because I've never experienced bitter chill like this for such an extended length of time. My teeth chatter and I feel the puffs of frost exhaling at each breath. I sleep intermittently until howls and scratching claws wake me, like raindrops of horror splashing on my brain. When I wake, I try to rub the numbness from my feet and hands so frostbite does not set in. How much longer can I survive? How much longer do I *want* to survive?

How much longer will it take this part of the world to freeze completely? Another month? A year until we slip across a mantle of solid ice?

The creatures do not seem affected by the biting cold, as if they've adapted like arctic wolves. Whatever viral infection or evolutionary mutation caused them to transform to beasts in the first place, bred the means for survival in this new world, evolving appendages with massive leather pads and coating skin in thick blankets of fur. Perhaps it was arranged all along, evolution working to modify us for survival as it sensed the slowing of the universe. Perhaps other species in other lands have been slowly developing adaptations for this event, hiding mutations in their DNA. I think of fish that live far under the glaciers of Antarctica, where no plant life or sunlight ever reaches. They flourish below, while perhaps the werewolves may flourish above. For all I know, the demon dogs have been slated for the top rung of evolution's master plan all along.

I wonder at these things as I lie alone in the dark, in the cold.

My watch still labors onward and, if I listen closely, each second sounds a quiet pulse, a bond for my own heart to beat: tick, tick, tick . . . If that watch should cease, I know I would, too. I wind my watch each day, in consideration of that, and I pray the great horologist of the universe should do the same just one last time. My prayers are not answered. It seems futile of me to continue winding my watch as the seconds of my life count down. Maybe that horologist thought the same as he lay trapped and dying in his own wine cellar, or maybe I *am* the horologist and the microcosm that considers me their center will perish, wondering *why*?

I believe madness seeps into my brain, carried along by flurries of terror and chill, and I wish desperately to see the radiance of the beautiful moon again.

I blindly feel around the floor until my hands grasp the bottle of sleeping pills. I shake them and listen to the rattle of capsules against each other like the dry seeds of a gourd. The werewolves howl and pound at the door. I could consume the pills and be done with it all; peace would whisper upon me and perhaps a final moment of warmth. I would die alone in the dark of the cellar.

I curse the absurdity of it all and wish suddenly: Oh, to be a wolf-man now and live free under the full light of the moon, to run wild in the companionship of a pack! To no longer wonder if death would come from frost or starvation or worse.

Would they devour me, should I give myself to them? Or would they be merciful, my neighbors and friends, and turn me to one of their own? Do they know more than I?

Perhaps they recognize who I am, and the beasts are only trying to help, to save me. They pound on the door calling for me to come out so they may rescue me from this dying human form.

Is madness deceiving me or has my watch already stopped ticking? Should I take the pills or go outside? I gasp and my muscles spasm as the cold constricts with icy fingers. I would weep, but the tears turn to icicles on my lashes. I think of the dark and the light beyond.

Last night, I opened the cellar door ...

CAR TRIP BINGO

(*First American Publishing)

by Eric J. Guignard

T THAT BIG OL' SUN IS SO ROUND, YELLOW, AND flat it looks like Mom's hat the time she sat on it. Everyone had laughed, 'cept for her, but then after awhile she laughed too. That was a long time ago.

And that big ol' sun is right in front of us, filling the highway as if we're driving right into it, though I know we're not, unless Dad is tricking us again. Dad's like that, saying one day we're driving to China, the next day to Mars, the next day to home. We don't go any of those places.

"Hanged Men," Maddy announces.

Maddy's my older brother and he's buckled in next to me, smacking gum and blowing bubbles. One bursts every couple of minutes, sounding like a wet towel snapping your butt, the way they used to in gym class.

"Where?" I ask, staring through my window, but before Maddy responds they come into view around a curve in the highway, stretching amongst a line of tangled telephone poles. Maddy's angle in the car had just let him get a glimpse before me. "Never mind, I see 'em."

Maddy crosses the image of Hanged Men off his card where it falls under the letter N. Each of our cards has five boxes across by five boxes down, filled with different illustrations. I've only got two boxes marked off my card, while Maddy's crossed out four, including the latest, but all of his are marked in separate columns.

I turn back as we pass some amazing dunes, the crests shifting in slight wind to hint at the cities buried below. The dunes are mostly volcanic ash, but Dad said they're also part desert sand and part pulverized bone. I just think it's cool when crest after crest flows in ripples under the sun like golden ocean waves.

There's flapping across the horizon of huge white wings, and after a moment of scrutiny, I announce, "Gigantic Roc!"

"Where?" Maddy asks, and I point to the horrible bird of prey. Maddy's lip curls down, pulling a strand of gum with it. "I thought those didn't exist."

"Well, there it is." I mark it off my card.

I barely have time to bask in my latest find before he calls, "Blood funnel!"

"Where?"

"Behind that air dirigible."

"The blimp with the stars and letters all over it?"

"It's the only one in the sky, doofus."

"Maddy . . ." Dad warns in his big voice.

"Sorry."

"All right, I see the blood funnel." It really is hard to miss, opening a great sucking whirl through the heavens, but I'd been focusing on the dunes and roc in the other direction. The funnel sucks in the dirigible like flicking a piece of popcorn into your mouth, and Maddy marks it off his card.

Our sister, Baby June, should be sitting between me and Maddy, but she's not, which is why Maddy's next to me. Baby June's car seat is empty, looking kinda like an empty socket when a tooth's fallen out. I know 'cause I've still got three missing teeth, all in the back of my mouth. Baby June's not missing like my teeth or anything, just sleeping in Mom's arms, since she cries a lot if she doesn't get enough attention, and Maddy and I are too busy playing games to be fussing over her.

And Mom and Dad sit up front as usual. Dad's the one who drives all the time, and Mom reads the maps, or pretends to read, since she stopped giving Dad directions sometime ago. I guess that doesn't matter, since he always acts like he knows where we're going.

Now to our left—past the crumbling guardrail—a foamy green ocean crashes against cliffs that rise so high you can never see their peaks. Old iron ships with red funnels and sharp prows are smashed against the bluffs, then the tide drags them back until the next surge catches them to smash into the bluffs again.

"Why did so many ships sail into the cliffs?" I ask.

"I'm sure they didn't mean to," Dad answers. "Mountains weren't always there."

"How'd the captains and sailors get rescued?"

"I doubt they ever did, son."

"I bet it's like a roller coaster ride for them," Maddy adds. "Back and forth, up and down."

I review my card for Doomed Vessels, but it isn't there. At least it's not on Maddy's card either.

"Should've seen it back in sixty-eight," Dad says. "Caught a whole company of whalers." He looks at us in reverse through the rearview mirror, and Maddy whistles appreciatively, though I think it's only because he feels expected to do so. The whistle interrupts his snapping gum at least.

Maddy glances at me, then to the window. "Dead bird!"

"Where?" I crane my neck trying to glimpse out Maddy's side of the car.

"Up there," he points to the blue and bronze sky.

I gaze out, but all I see are fuzzy clouds that look like fingers pointing our way. "I don't see them."

"Gotcha!" Maddy laughs. "How could a dead bird be up in the sky? Ha ha!"

Dad laughs too, but Mom doesn't say anything, just holds Baby June.

I feel the heat turning my cheeks crimson. When I turn back to my seat though, I catch glimpse of a monstrous yellow orb winking open from the distance.

"Sentinel Eye, Sentinel Eye!" I yell excitedly.

"Where?" Maddy asks, turning his head every direction.

"Back there, behind us!"

"Good one," Dad says.

If we were nearer, Dad would worry us about lasers shooting from the eye's double-ringed pupils or else de—*dem*—

"Dad, what's that word, when you're evaporated from staring into the Sentinel Eye?"

"Dematerialization, son."

"That's it, thanks.

Dad would worry us about dematerialization, but the eye is too far away to cause concern. I mean, to it, we're just some dumb dust mote floating away.

I cross its image off my card, under the letter G.

Johnny jumps up suddenly from the seat behind us, and Maddy's bubble bursts. It startles me, but the seatbelt keeps me from leaping up, though my heart feels like I dropped down a slide. Johnny barks and sticks his head out an open window to snap at swarms of those little honeybees that turn purple at dusk. He might have gotten a couple, but then a giant dragonfly dives down and reaches for him with a pair of hairy forelegs. Johnny yips real loud and jumps back down under the seat with his tail curled tight. We all laugh, except for Mom of course, and Dad pushes the button that makes the window go up.

"We sure don't want *that* in here!" he says, winking in the rearview.

Maddy and I both look over our cards for Mutant Dragonfly, but neither of us has it. A comet shoots across the sky and collides with the sun, and there's a tiny flare of red like watching a pimple form and pop in high speed.

Johnny must have woken up Grandma, because her voice yells from behind me, "Are we there yet?"

Dad sighs. "No, Mom, it'll probably still be awhile."

"I gotta tinkle," she yells. Grandma always yells, since she can't hear properly, and she forgot her listening aid at home.

"I told you to go before we left."

"I did . . . I gotta go again. We've been driving since before Hoover wore panties."

That must've been an old-person joke because Grandpa mutters, "I told you before, don't slander Hoover."

"You and Hoover, you and Hoover," Grandma taunts. "Should've married him 'stead of me. Let's see Hoover change your damned diapers."

We all cringe. Grandma wouldn't have dared say such things before, but when the First Realignments occurred—when the end-of-world scenarios began overlapping—Grandpa had a stroke and fell, and now he's paralyzed below the neck. Before that he was a marine and big in politics, and he told everyone what to do all the time. Now he mostly eats yogurt.

Dad cuts in, "Mom, just use a water bottle."

"Can't we take a stop for five minutes?"

"You know the answer to that."

She sighs the same way Dad sighs, and a moment later I hear a swish of clothing and then a long splash.

I gaze back out my window and watch fields of scarlet poppies rustle in the wind, overrunning the ruins of naked ivory statues that are all missing arms or heads. The flowers attract small birds, which in turn attract more of the mutant dragonflies, and it's all so pretty and peaceful, and I love how the sun makes each of the flowers seem to sparkle like little red jewels. Not far away, the skeleton of a great bridge rises in the backdrop until reaching a center pylon that's been sheared in half. Frayed cables dance back and forth around it like sky snakes.

We've turned inland away from the ocean, but the big ol' sun still fills the road ahead, so maybe that means we didn't make the turn from the ocean, but the coastline turned from us. That happens sometimes.

Baby June makes a gurgling cry, then coos. Mom pats her on the back, then caresses June's face, silently, always silently. I consider maybe it's Mom who needs Baby June more than the other way around.

"Berserker Tank!" Maddy yells.

"Where?" me and Dad both ask at the same time, but for different reasons.

"Over there."

Maddy points across an access road, and I see the dread war machine, a double turreted fortress trundling along on eight treads and the sweat of two hundred slaves. A flash illuminates the sky, and one turret recoils as it fires a pulse against some barb-wired bulwark that still flies a lonely city flag. The bulwark and flag and surrounding land vanish.

Dad nudges down the gas pedal a little more and we accelerate away.

"Darn it," Maddy says. "I thought that was on my card."

"It's on mine!" I reply, and lift my pencil to cross it off.

"No, that doesn't count. I saw the Berserker Tank first," he complains.

"But if it's not on your card, then the option to cross it off goes to me."

"No it doesn't! That's Novikov Self-Consistency rules. We're playing by Gödel Metrics."

"But that allows global caus—*caus* . . . what's that word, Dad?"

"Causality violation," Dad says. "But that's a precedent you have to decide in advance of playing if you're going to accept or not. Maddy's right, you can't just choose theoretical models in the middle of a game."

"Aw."

To his credit, Maddy doesn't gloat. He just snaps another bubble.

Patches of snow and moss begin to dot the shoulder of the road, and we pass more than one wrecked car that's spun out or been stepped on by behemoths. Colorful scenery flies by, faster and faster, and it's easy to image we were the ones at a standstill and everything else is speeding by, instead of us, the ones always moving.

"We need some music," cousin Skip says, sitting a couple rows behind Grandma and Grandpa.

"What you listen to ain't music," Grandma yells.

"Just use your headphones," Dad orders in his big voice. "The boys are playing."

Johnny yips agreement. Skip doesn't say anything else, just sulks, which is what he's good at. It's easy to forget Skip is back there when he's silent. It's easy to forget about all the others behind us, involved in their own games or dreams or whatever else they do to pass the time while we drive. Some have been silent so long, they'll probably never speak again.

"Guardian Walls!" I announce.

"Where?"

"On top of that hill."

"Those ruins? They aren't guarding anything."

Maddy's right that the walls are in ruin, steel and brick pockmarked with shell holes, and snapping lizards running free through smoldering fissures. The force field generator tower is swamped in oozing pink mold while bobbing tentacles extend through its apertures. Still... I catch glimpse of a Guardian charging along its medieval embrasure, swinging his plasma sword at a nest of ox-spiders.

"It's still manned," I argue.

Maddy snaps a bubble in admission. "Okay."

I mark it off my card. "Whoa! That's four in a row under the letter G. One more and I win!"

"Beginner's luck," Maddy says. He still has more boxes marked off than me, but his are scattered in twos and threes beneath each letter. "Even if you win this game, I still won at Foldovers and Tic-Tac-Toe, so that would make me the overall winner."

"Maddy, don't be a spoil sport," Dad says.

"Car Trip Bingo is better anyway," I say. "So that counts more than the other games combined."

"I wouldn't be so anxious to win," Dad tells me.

"Why not?"

"When someone claims *Bingo*, that's the end of our car trip."

"Where'll we be when that happens?"

"Our destination."

"Oh." I look to Mom for clarification, but she doesn't say anything, just stares out the windshield.

"I don't want our trip to end yet."

"Nothing *I* can do about it, son." His reverse look comes from the mirror. "It's just a game, isn't it?"

"I'm hungry," someone whines from far behind. "I wanna use the restroom."

"Mom, could you pass back your bottle?" Dad says to Grandma. He adds to us, "Bet that one's on one of your cards."

"It *is*! Row N!" Maddy says. "Just like our prisoner—see, there's Unhappy Captive below the N!"

We all laugh, except for Mom. It's funny because the rows in the car go back so far we just started naming them by letters, and it's row 'N' where the prisoner's at, the same as the row on Maddy's card.

Maddy crosses it off. "Hey, that makes four for me under the letter N. Now either of us can win!"

Way off, purple storm clouds rise above a dark forest, and lightning bolts flash, but it's all so faint and at odds against the lush green jungle vines and Siamese panthers that now fill our view. *Either of us can win . . .*

I consider the card again and its last image under the letter G, all the way down at the bottom of the column: *Galactic Reversal.*

I consider too, that big ol' sun that's still so pretty and filling the highway like we're driving right into it, and I wonder if we keep going, would we make it there?

I exchange glances with Maddy, knowing he thinks like me, and he crumples up his card and tosses it out the window.

We don't want it to end.

"Do over."

EDITOR'S REQUEST

DEAR READER, FAN, OR SUPPORTER,

It's a dreadful commentary that the worth of indie publications is measured by online 5-star reviews, but such is the state of current commerce.

Should you have enjoyed this book, gratitude is most appreciated by posting a brief and honest online review at Amazon.com, Goodreads.com, and/or a highly-visible blog.

With sincerest thanks,

Eric J. Guignard, editor
Strange Tales of the Macabre: Post-Apocalyptic

ALSO EDITED BY ERIC J. GUIGNARD:

A WORLD OF HORROR

Every nation of the globe has unique tales to tell, whispers that settle in through the land, creatures or superstitions that enliven the night, but rarely do readers get to experience such a diversity of these voices in one place as in *A WORLD OF HORROR*, the latest anthology book created by award-winning editor Eric J. Guignard, and beautifully illustrated by artist Steve Lines.

Enclosed within its pages are twenty-two all-new dark and speculative fiction stories written by authors from around the world that explore the myths and monsters, fables and fears of their homelands.

Encounter the haunting things that stalk those radioactive forests outside Chernobyl in Ukraine; sample the curious dishes one may eat in Canada; beware the veldt monster that mirrors yourself in Uganda; or simply battle mountain trolls alongside Alfred Nobel in Sweden. These stories and more are found within *A World of Horror*: Enter and discover, truly, there's no place on the planet devoid of frights, thrills, and wondrous imagination.

"This breath of fresh air for horror readers shows the limitless possibilities of the genre."
　　　　　　　　　　　　　　　—*Publishers Weekly* (starred review)

"This is the book we need right now!"
　　　　　　　　　　　　　　　—*Becky Spratford; librarian, reviewer,* RA for All: Horror

"A fresh collection of horror authors exploring monsters and myths from their homelands."

　　　　　　　　　　　　　　　　　　　　　　　　—*Library Journal*

Order your copy at www.darkmoonbooks.com or www.amazon.com
ISBN-13: 978-0-9885569-2-8

ALSO EDITED BY ERIC J. GUIGNARD:

THE FIVE SENSES OF HORROR

Hearing, sight, touch, smell, and taste: Our impressions of the world are formed by our five senses, and so too are our fears, our imaginations, and our captivation in reading fiction stories that embrace these senses.

Whether hearing the song of infernal caverns, tasting the erotic kiss of treachery, or smelling the lush fragrance of a fiend, enclosed within this anthology are fifteen horror and dark fantasy tales that will quicken the beat of fear, sweeten the flavor of wonder, sharpen the spike of thrills, and otherwise brighten the marvel of storytelling that is found resonant!

Editor Eric J. Guignard and psychologist Jessica Bayliss, PhD also include companion discourse throughout, offering academic and literary insight as well as psychological commentary examining the physiology of our senses, why each of our senses are engaged by dark fiction stories, and how it all inspires writers to continually churn out ideas in uncommon and invigorating ways.

Featuring stunning interior illustrations by Nils Bross, and including fiction short stories by such world-renowned authors as John Farris, Ramsey Campbell, Poppy Z. Brite, Darrell Schweitzer, and Richard Christian Matheson, amongst others.

Intended for readers, writers, and students alike, explore *THE FIVE SENSES OF HORROR*!

Order your copy at www.darkmoonbooks.com or www.amazon.com
ISBN-13: 978-0-9988275-0-6

ALSO EDITED BY ERIC J. GUIGNARD:

POP THE CLUTCH: THRILLING TALES OF ROCKABILLY, MONSTERS, AND HOT ROD HORROR

Welcome to the cool side of the 1950s, where the fast cars and revved-up movie monsters peel out in the night. Where outlaw vixens and jukebox tramps square off with razorblades and lead pipes. Where rockers rock, cool cats strut, and hot rods roar. Where you howl to the moon as the tiki drums pound and the electric guitar shrieks and that spit-and-holler jamboree ain't gonna stop for a long, long time . . . maybe never.

This is the '50s where ghost shows still travel the back roads of the south, and rockabilly has a hold on the nation's youth; where lucky hearts tell the tale, and maybe that fella in the Shriners' fez ain't so square after all. Where exist noir detectives of the supernatural, tattoo artists of another kind, Hollywood fix-it men, and a punk kid with grasshopper arms under his chain-studded jacket and an icy stare on his face.

This is the '50s of *Pop the Clutch: Thrilling Tales of Rockabilly, Monsters, and Hot Rod Horror*. This is your ticket to the dark side of American kitsch . . . the fun and frightful side!

"A fitting tribute to the 1950s with this 18-story compendium of hot rods, rock 'n' roll, and creature features come to life."

—*Publishers Weekly*

Order your copy at www.darkmoonbooks.com or www.amazon.com
ISBN-13: 978-0-9834335-9-0

ALSO EDITED BY ERIC J. GUIGNARD:

Death. Who has not considered their own mortality and wondered at what awaits, once our frail human shell expires? What occurs after the heart stops beating, after the last breath is drawn, after life as we know it terminates?

Does our spirit remain on Earth while the body rots? Do the remnants of our soul transcend to a celestial Heaven or sink to Hell's torment? Can we choose our own afterlife? Can we die again in the hereafter? Are we given the opportunity to reincarnate and do it all over? Is life merely a cosmic joke or is it an experiment for something greater? Enclosed in this Bram Stoker-award winning anthology are thirty-four all-new dark and speculative fiction stories exploring the possibilities *AFTER DEATH . . .*

Illustrated by Audra Phillips and including stories by: **Steve Rasnic Tem, Bentley Little, John Langan, Simon Clark, Lisa Morton, Joe McKinney, Ray Cluley, David Tallerman,** and exceptional others.

"Though the majority of the pieces come from the darker side of the genre, a solid minority are playful, clever, or full of wonder. This strong anthology is sure to make readers contemplative even while it creates nightmares."
—*Publishers Weekly*

"In Eric J. Guignard's latest anthology he gathers some of the biggest and most talented authors on the planet to give us their take on this entertaining and perplexing subject matter . . . highly recommended."
—*Famous Monsters of Filmland*

"An excellent collection of imaginative tales of what waits beyond the veil."
—*Amazing Stories Magazine*

Order your copy at www.darkmoonbooks.com or www.amazon.com
ISBN-13: 978-0-9885569-2-8

ALSO EDITED BY ERIC J. GUIGNARD:

Darkness exists everywhere, and in no place greater than those where spirits and curses still reside. Tread not lightly on ancient lands that have been discovered by this collection of intrepid authors.

In **DARK TALES OF LOST CIVILIZATIONS**, you will unearth an anthology of twenty-five previously unpublished horror and speculative fiction stories, relating to aspects of civilizations that are crumbling, forgotten, rediscovered, or perhaps merely spoken about in great and fearful whispers.

What is it that lures explorers to distant lands where none have returned? Where is Genghis Khan buried? What happened to Atlantis? Who will displace mankind on Earth? What laments have the Witches of Oz? Answers to these mysteries and other tales are presented within this critically acclaimed anthology.

Including stories by: **Joe R. Lansdale, David Tallerman, Jonathan Vos Post, Jamie Lackey, Aaron J. French**, and twenty exceptional others.

"The stories range from mildly disturbing to downright terrifying . . . Most are written in a conservative, suggestive style, relying on the reader's own imagination to take the plunge from speculation to horror."
—*Monster Librarian Reviews*

"Several of these stories made it on to my best of the year shortlist, and the book itself is now on the best anthologies of the year shortlist."
—*British Fantasy Society*

"Almost any story in this anthology is worth the price of purchase. The entire collection is a delight."
—*Black Gate Magazine*

ALSO CREATED BY ERIC J. GUIGNARD:

EXPLORING DARK SHORT FICTION #1: A PRIMER TO STEVE RASNIC TEM

For over four decades, Steve Rasnic Tem has been an acclaimed author of horror, weird, and sentimental fiction. Hailed by *Publishers Weekly* as "A perfect balance between the bizarre and the straight-forward" and *Library Journal* as "One of the most distinctive voices in imaginative literature," Steve Rasnic Tem has been read and cherished the world over for his affecting, genre-crossing tales.

Dark Moon Books and editor Eric J. Guignard bring you this introduction to his work, the first in a series of primers exploring modern masters of literary dark short fiction. Herein is a chance to discover—or learn more of—the rich voice of Steve Rasnic Tem, as beautifully illustrated by artist Michelle Prebich.

Included within these pages are:
- Six short stories, one written exclusively for this book
- Author interview
- Complete bibliography
- Academic commentary by Michael Arnzen, PhD (former humanities chair and professor of the year, Seton Hill University)
- …and more!

Enter this doorway to the vast and fantastic: Get to know Steve Rasnic Tem.

Order your copy at www.darkmoonbooks.com or www.amazon.com
ISBN-13: 978-0-9988275-2-0

ALSO CREATED BY ERIC J. GUIGNARD:

EXPLORING DARK SHORT FICTION #2:
A PRIMER TO KAARON WARREN

Australian author Kaaron Warren is widely recognized as one of the leading writers today of speculative and dark short fiction. She's published four novels, multiple novellas, and well over one hundred heart-rending tales of horror, science fiction, and beautiful fantasy, and is the first author ever to simultaneously win all three of Australia's top speculative fiction writing awards (Ditmar, Shadows, and Aurealis awards for *The Grief Hole*).

Dark Moon Books and editor Eric J. Guignard bring you this introduction to her work, the second in a series of primers exploring modern masters of literary dark short fiction. Herein is a chance to discover—or learn more of—the distinct voice of Kaaron Warren, as beautifully illustrated by artist Michelle Prebich.

Included within these pages are:
- Six short stories, one written exclusively for this book
- Author interview
- Complete bibliography
- Academic commentary by Michael Arnzen, PhD (former humanities chair and professor of the year, Seton Hill University)
- . . . and more!

Enter this doorway to the vast and fantastic: Get to know Kaaron Warren.

Order your copy at www.darkmoonbooks.com or www.amazon.com
ISBN-13: 978-0-9989383-0-1

ALSO CREATED BY ERIC J. GUIGNARD:

EXPLORING DARK SHORT FICTION #3:
A PRIMER TO NISI SHAWL

Praised by both literary journals and leading fiction magazines, Nisi Shawl is celebrated as an author whose works are lyrical and philosophical, speculative and far-ranging; "...broad in ambition and deep in accomplishment" (*The Seattle Times*). Besides nearly three decades of creating fantasy and science fiction, fairy tales, and indigenous stories, Nisi has also been lauded as editor, journalist, and proponent of feminism, African-American fiction, and other pedagogical issues of diversity.

Dark Moon Books and editor Eric J. Guignard bring you this introduction to her work, the third in a series of primers exploring modern masters of literary dark short fiction. Herein is a chance to discover—or learn more of—the vibrant voice of Nisi Shawl, as beautifully illustrated by artist Michelle Prebich.

Included within these pages are:
- Six short stories, one written exclusively for this book
- Author interview
- Complete bibliography
- Academic commentary by Michael Arnzen, PhD (former humanities chair and professor of the year, Seton Hill University)
- ...and more!

Enter this doorway to the vast and fantastic: Get to know Nisi Shawl.

Order your copy at www.darkmoonbooks.com or www.amazon.com
ISBN-13: 978-0-9989383-4-9

THE CRIME FILES OF KATY GREEN by GENE O'NEILL:

Discover why readers have been applauding this stark, fast-paced noir series by multiple-award-winning author, Gene O'Neill, and follow the dark murder mysteries of Sacramento homicide detectives Katy Green and Johnny Cato, dubbed by the press as Sacramento's "Green Hornet and Cato"!

Book #1: DOUBLE JACK (a novella)

400-pound serial killer Jack Malenko has discovered the perfect cover: He dresses as a CalTrans worker and preys on female motorists in distress in full sight of passing traffic. How fast can Katy Green and Johnny Cato track him down before he strikes again?

ISBN-13: 978-0-9988275-6-8

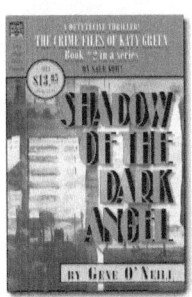

Book #2: SHADOW OF THE DARK ANGEL

Bullied misfit, Samuel Kubiak, is visited by a dark guardian angel who helps Samuel gain just vengeance. There hasn't been a case yet Katy and Johnny haven't solved, but now how can they track a psychopathic suspect that comes and goes in the shadows?

ISBN-13: 978-0-9988275-8-2

Book #3: DEATHFLASH

Billy Williams can see the soul as it departs the body, and is "commanded to do the Lord's work," which he does fanatically, slaying drug addicts in San Francisco...Katy and Johnny investigate the case as junkies die all around, for Billy has his own addiction: the rush of viewing the *Deathflash*.

ISBN-13: 978-0-9988275-9-9

Order your copy at www.darkmoonbooks.com or www.amazon.com

ABOUT THE CONTRIBUTORS

KATE JONEZ

Dark fantasy and horror author Kate Jonez has twice been nominated for the Bram Stoker Award® and once for the Shirley Jackson. Her short fiction has appeared in *The Best Horror of the Year*, *Black Static*, *Pseudopod*, *Gamut*, and *Haunted Nights* edited by Ellen Datlow and Lisa Morton. Her collection *Lady Bits* published by Trepidatio, an imprint of JournalStone is available at journalstone.com/bookstore/lady-bits/.

She is also the chief editor at the Bram Stoker Award®-winning small press Omnium Gatherum, which is dedicated to publishing unique dark fantasy, weird fiction, and horror.

Kate is a student of all things scary, and when she isn't writing she loves to collect objects for her cabinet of curiosities, research obscure and strange historical figures, and explore Southern California where she lives with a very nice man and two little dogs who are also very nice but could behave a little bit better.

Find more about her here: www.katejonez.com.

RENA MASON

Rena Mason is a three-time Bram Stoker Award® winning author of the *The Evolutionist* and *East End Girls*, as well as a 2014 Stage 32/The Blood List Presents®: The Search for New Blood Screenwriting Contest Quarter-Finalist. She's had nearly two dozen short stories, novelettes, and novellas published in various award-winning anthologies and magazines and writes a monthly *Haunted Travels* column. A longtime fan of horror, sci-fi, science, history, historical fiction, mysteries, and thrillers, she began writing to mash up those genres in stories revolving around everyday life.

She is a member of the Horror Writers Association, Mystery Writers of America, International Thriller Writers, The International Screenwriters' Association, and the Public Safety Writers Association.

An R.N. and avid scuba diver, she has traveled the world and incorporates the experiences into her stories. She currently resides in Reno, Nevada with her family.

For more information about this author, check out her website: www.RenaMason.Ink

Follow her on Twitter: @RenaMason88

Facebook: www.facebook.com/rena.mason

LISA MORTON

Lisa Morton is a novelist, screenwriter, author of non-fiction books, and six-time winner of the Bram Stoker Award® whose work was described by the American Library Association's *Readers' Advisory Guide to Horror* as "consistently dark, unsettling, and frightening". Her most recent release, *Ghost Stories: Classic Tales of Horror and Suspense* (co-edited with Leslie S. Klinger), was called "a work of art" by *Publishers Weekly* (starred review). Forthcoming short fiction appearances include *Ten Terrifying Tales to Tell at Night* (Simon & Schuster), *The Lovecraft Squad: Rising* (Pegasus), and the first issue of the rebooted *Weird Tales magazine;* and a new nonfiction book, *Calling the Spirits: A History of Seances* (Reaktion Books). Lisa lives in the San Fernando Valley and online at www.lisamorton.com.

JOHN PALISANO

John Palisano has a pair of books with Samhain Publishing, *Dust of the Dead* and *Ghost Heart*. *Nerves* is available through Bad Moon Books. *Starlight Drive: Four Halloween Tales* was released in time for Halloween, and his first short fiction collection *All That Withers* is available from Cycatrix press, celebrating over a decade of short story highlights. *Night of 1,000 Beasts* is also now available.

He won the Bram Stoker Award® in short fiction in 2016 for "Happy Joe's Rest Stop". More short stories have appeared in anthologies from Cemetery Dance, PS Publishing, Independent Legions, DarkFuse, Crystal Lake, Terror Tales, Lovecraft eZine, Horror Library, Bizarro Pulp, Written Backwards, Dark Continents, Big Time Books, McFarland Press, Darkscribe, Dark House, Omnium Gatherum, and more.

Non-fiction pieces have appeared in *Blumhouse*, *Fangoria*, *Backstreets*, and *Dark Discoveries* magazines.

He is currently serving as the President of the Horror Writers Association.

Say 'hi' at: www.johnpalisano.com and http://www.amazon.com/author/johnpalisano and www.facebook.com/johnpalisano and www.twitter.com/johnpalisano

ERIC J. GUIGNARD

Eric J. Guignard has twice won the Bram Stoker Award® (the highest literary award of horror fiction), been a finalist for the International Thriller Writers Award, and a multi-nominee of the Pushcart Prize for his works of dark and speculative fiction. He has over one hundred stories and non-fiction credits appearing in publications around the world and has edited multiple anthologies. Through his indie press, Dark Moon Books, he currently publishes the acclaimed series of author primers created to champion modern masters of the dark and macabre, *Exploring Dark Short Fiction*, and through SourceBooks he curates the new series, *The Horror Writers Association Presents: Haunted Library of Horror Classics* with co-editor Leslie S. Klinger. Out now is his story collection, *That Which Grows Wild* (Cemetery Dance) and novel, *Doorways To The Deadeye* (JournalStone). For more, visit Eric at: www.ericjguignard.com or Twitter: @ericjguignard.